Morocco and earthquakes seen through my glasses

A different Morocco from the travel agencies

Poul Otto Jorgensen

Morocco and earthquakes seen through my glasses

A different Morocco from the travel agencies

Poul Otto Jorgensen

Morocco and earthquakes seen through my glasses
© 2024 Poul Otto Jorgensen
Publisher: BoD • Books on Demand GmbH, In de Tarpen 42,
22848 Norderstedt, Tyskland
Manufacturing/printing: Libri Plureos GmbH, Friedensallee 273,
22763 Hamborg, Tyskland
Translation: Poul Otto Jorgensen
ISBN: 978-87-4305-923-3

Contents

Preface

I spend a lot of time in Morocco, where I am married to the Berber woman, Jamila. We live in a mountain area in the village of Hay Assersif, which is near a larger town, called Aourir, located approximately 20 km from Agadir.

When I am in Morocco, I often talk to the people about Morocco and the different areas, each with their own distinctive character. When I drink my tea with nana (mint), I get to know many things ranging from geography, population composition, occupations, government systems and family relationships and much more. Regarding family relationships, you have to be careful, because in the Berber area where I am, I have learned that many people are related to each other. "Well, I know your wife well because my mother is her cousin!" I was told once, and it was not the last time. Sometimes when we go to Aourir and my wife greets someone I might already know, I say: "Where do you know her from!" Well, that's my aunt!" says Jamila. The family is like brothers and sisters, they can say bad things about each other; but if I interfere, I get the "hat pool."

Although all those I have talked to and talk to about Morocco probably do not think how much and great information they have given me, I would like to thank them very much, because without their help it would not have been possible to write this book.

I would especially like to thank my little Berber wife Jamila. Subsequent thanks must go to my friends mentioned in no particular order: Soufiane, Hassan, my brother-in-law Mohamed, Ahmed and Aaziz. I have purposely not mentioned their last names as I know they won't care.

Furthermore, my late brother Henning Jorgensen's reports have been an invaluable help. He often told about the Morocco he traveled sparsely, when he worked in Morocco, where he also had many acquaintances from high to low.

In the vast majority of places in the book, I have primarily quoted my wife Jamila, friends or brother; where I have lacked years or information about circumstances etc., I have used Wikipedia Maroc, Wikipedia Histoire du Sahara Occidental and Wikipedia History of Western Sahara. I have subsequently checked all the information with my expert friends just for the record. In addition, I often read Morocco World News, which rubs off on me.

I would also like to point out that it is not the UN as an organization that I am complaining about in the book; for the intentions at the creation of the United Nations were noble and noble for the welfare of mankind.

But there must be something better than the right of veto, which hampers many initiatives and hampers much work. I have never considered the right of veto democratic. The heavy administration could be made much easier, practical and more down-to-earth. It would also be nice if the better-informed older brother let his younger siblings speak more. As the old hippie told me: "The UN is like an octopus with too many arms and too much ink!"

But back to Morocco!

I drove through the Anti-Atlas mountains and visited Ouarzazate, Zagora and the Sahara desert, which is what we call the Sahara (sahara really just means desert in Arabic) in January 2013. Jamila and I repeated the expedition a few years later, as described in my book "The Old Map;' where we were lucky to find the treasure that the old, yellow, faded map showed us the way to.

We have also traveled by bus to Marrakech and further by both bus and train up through Morocco to Casablanca and Rabat and been to the old, formerly Portuguese city of Essaouira several times.

In addition, I have gradually gained a great knowledge of Agadir and the surrounding towns.

Before I start, I better say that the spellings I use are the spellings used in Morocco in names etc. An example: In Denmark you write

Muhammed, in Morocco you write Mohamed. It wouldn't be so nice if too many writing experts came after me.

I also hope for your mercy and understanding for translation and grammar! I am Danish and have translated this little book myself in the hope that the price can be kept down, so that it can reach as many people as possible.

Introduction

I am in Sweden at the moment (2023) and intend to return to Morocco in the middle of August. I just opened the Mondley app to keep up my language skills. Every day I read a bit of French and a bit of classical Arabic and also practice a bit of Spanish.

But we have to start somewhere, so let's start with the presentation of the Morocco map I've "knitted together," without listing too many cities, so it's easy to keep track of where we are in Morocco. It's handy to know where things are without too much confusion.

Next, we look at Morocco's history and language with the facts and years that are necessary. We must also look at Morocco's population. It is all seasoned with my own experiences and experiences.

Morocco card

History and Language of Morocco

As I have already expressed, during my stays in Morocco I have absorbed the glories right from 2012, when I came to the country for the first time.

On my very first expedition in the Anti-Atlas mountains, Ouarzazate, Zagora and the Sahara desert, I discovered how different a country Morocco is. It is diverse both in terms of landscape, population and culture.

I remember from my schooling that the area up north by the Mediterranean is an ancient highly cultural area that had both Phoenicia and Carthage as trading partners. Later, the area came under Roman rule, like so many other countries in the world at the time.

I have also learned that much human behavior in Morocco is different from several of the Arab countries, and I attribute this to the phenomenon that Morocco was never occupied by the Ottomans, as most of the other countries along the Mediterranean coast were. Why Morocco went free, I don't know. But a guess could be the Atlas and Anti-Atlas mountains with the original "wild" inhabitants. The Romans called them the barbarians, as they called all foreign people they did not know. Over time, the word barbar has become Berber.

Briefly, although France was on a conquest spree in the 19th century in North Africa, Morocco was not conquered, probably to avoid stepping on Spain's toes, as Spain had interests in the area. But in 1912 something happened anyway. Northern Morocco became a Spanish protectorate and today constitutes the areas of Ceuta and Melilla; Ceuta is on the Strait of Gibraltar and Melilla is on the east coast of Morocco on the Mediterranean. The rest of Morocco became a French protectorate with the exception of Western Sahara, which came under Spanish rule under the name Rio de Oro or Spanish Sahara.

The French were efficient, new roads had to be built and infrastructure had to be maximized so they could get the most out of the colony. The population was discharged for forced labor; yes even "our grandmother", who was a young efficient woman at the time, came to work, she was appointed road foreman due to her good organizational sense and determination.

The population of Morocco at the time revolted, which the occupying powers tried to put down. In 1934, the insurgent had been defeated, it was believed.

But no fire without embers, it was still smoldering, so when a newly formed resistance organization became a reality, a well-functioning resistance struggle was launched.

When the sultan in the Moroccan area supported the rebels and supported a free Morocco, he was sent into exile by the French. As France lost their possessions in North Africa, so did Morocco, so in 1957 Morocco was transformed into a monarchy with the same Sultan as king under the name Mohamed V.

As can be almost calculated, there quickly became a conflict between the resistance organization – the national organization and the king; but wisely the king managed to hold the stronghold, which was succeeded by his son Hassan II on his death in 1961.

Much has been said about this king. In his own way, he was a hard man. He dissolved parliament in 1963, of course resulting in political unrest. It was not until 1970 that political parties were allowed again. Believe me or not, several parties went on strike, and they tried to overthrow Hassan II both in 1971 and in 1972.

My brother, who knew King Hassan II, has told several times what a capable king he was and admired him for the way he ruled Morocco, even if it was the harsh method. My brother said: "He was like King Solomon from the Old Testament!" The king was also admired for all the languages he spoke, many of which he spoke fluently.

When the Jews of Essaouira made a pilgrimage to the new Israel and many regretted it, they sent a deputation to Hassan II and gently asked about the possibility of coming back. Hassan II replied that since they had done nothing wrong, they were welcome back, so to this day the Jews and their way of life form a large part of the cityscape of Essaouira.

In 1975, King Hassan II and Morocco laid claim to the Spanish-occupied territory of Spanish Sahara or Western Sahara. The area is located far to the south in Morocco, next to the Atlantic Ocean. Morocco expressed that because of Western Sahara's historical affiliation with Morocco, it should be Moroccan. See the map page 10.

It ended with Morocco occupying a large part of the area; I have written much more about this in the chapter on Western Sahara.

The whole mess with the Spanish meant that relations between Spain and Morocco became/were bad.

The following little story testifies to how difficult it was to be a hated Spaniard in Morocco in those years. I should add before we start the story, that I have been under strict instructions from the family in question not to use real names, so the names I use in the story are fictitious.

Here comes the story: When the young Spanish sailor Juan XXX met the Berber girl Naïma YYY in Tangier, where she wanted to try her luck, sweet music arose and they fell in love. When they wanted to get married, was it not possible for a Moroccan woman to marry a Spanish man. But the otherwise strict bureaucracy and system in Morocco was nevertheless flexible and humane, so the solution was that Juan XXX converted his name to Mohamed ZZZ and became Moroccan. Now the two young people in love could finally get married.

The funny thing was that when Mohamed's/Juan's shipping company wrote or telegraphed to him, when he was at home with Naïma and the children from the see, his original name was written on the letters and telegrams. The same was the case with his Spanish family, they also used his original name when writing to him. But the Moroccan postal service was/is used to a bit of everything, so it went quite well.

When Juan died and Naïma was sent the pension from the shipping company every month, it was also his original name that appeared on the payments.

When King Hassan II died in 1999, his son became king with the name Mohamed VI.

Much has already been said and written about this king, who in my eyes is a fantastic king who understands Morocco's mixed population and its needs. He gradually delegates power in step with human development. He sends everyone to school and works to improve all conditions in general. But it takes time to change attitudes and understandings.

Try to look at the other states along the North African coast towards the Mediterranean, where hey wild animals were supposed to introduce democracy! The price of democracy can be too expensive!

It is therefore my great hope that King Mohamed VI will be given the opportunity to continue to rule the country in his sensible, pleasant and sensible way. He has understood how to form a bridge between Arabs, Berbers and the other minorities.

After some consideration, I have chosen to comment on the huge Berber demonstration that took place in Rabat on May 1 (2023), where Berbers drew attention to their lack of rights and lack of recognition of their language, and also expressed their great frustration at the lack of influence in state power.

Although the demonstration was against the constitution, it was not stopped! Why? I have answered: King Mohamed VI sits at the helm and acts in his sensible way, fortunately for that! I know I won't be popular in certain circles in my Morocco with that statement, but what's right must be right! As I have expressed before, the Berbers cannot find anyone else who works as well for their cause as King Mohamed VI. It was also expressed by his speech on June 30 (2023), where he commented on the demands of the Berbers and expressed that an institute of Berber culture will be established; the king also expressed that Berber culture and the Berbers are a national treasure.

I have no doubts at all about the king's real intentions and deep understanding of the Berbers, and I am absolutely sure that the day when the Berbers get their full vindication is not far off!

But as I have expressed it before, it takes time if you want to transform a society in a proper and good way. History shows that what I call "revolver democracies" are not for the well-being of the ordinary population.

I am well aware that the Berber movement has grown large; but I sincerely hope that the leaders it has do not "go overboard" and perform unintended and irreparable actions; but that they have the entire population of Morocco regardless of their ancestry in their hearts!

So when I sometimes meet rebellious individuals on my way who criticize the monarchy, I calmly explain to them how chaotic their lives would have been without King Mohamed VI at the helm.
Strangely enough, no one has yet been upset by my statements, on the contrary, they have led to many, long and matter-of-fact discussions.

Many of those I discuss with believe that democracy and the welfare state are the same. It can therefore be difficult to explain that you can live in a democracy without having a welfare society. When I explain, for example, how the Danish welfare society has crumbled over the last few years and tell about leg amputations that should never have taken place and about cancer operations that were never carried out, they don't believe me. But now I live with that.

The Berbers today learn their native language Tamazight, both written and spoken, in addition to Darija, which is spoken daily by the Arabs of Morocco. Darija is usually mistakenly called Arabic. "Real Arabic", classical Arabic is also part of the teaching at school.

While we are on the subject of languages there are three Berber languages, Tamazight language in Morocco. There is the Tamazigt of the Riefs in the north, there is the Tamazigt of the Berbers in the middle of Morocco and the Tamazigt of the Berbers in the south. According to my Berber wife Jamila, there is a difference between the three Berber languages, she believes that it must be like the difference between

15

Swedish and Danish.

But what are the characters like? These are letters called tifinagh, and fortunately they are fairly similar for all three Berber languages and are written like our Latin letters from left to right. They look like a wonderful amalgamation of all the letters we know from all over Europe. I immediately detect similarities between Greek letters and tifinagh. I have done some research into their origins and find that some believe, that the ancient Phoenician alphabet could be the origin.

Darija, as just written, is called Arabic by many in Morocco and even by several travel companies, despite the fact that it is incomprehensible to many Arabic-speaking people. I can best describe it with the following words spoken by an Iraqi who has a freeride residence in Agadir. He says, "Oh, the horrible language!" And I understand him! Because Darija is a mixed language, consisting of Arabic, the three Berber languages, French and a sprinkling of Spanish! When words are inflected, they are also inflected according to their origin. Darija is written in Arabic script from right to left.

One day, when I was talking to my friend the timber merchant and philosopher Soufiane, who has just taken a legal civil service exam, which he can't really start using, a whole load of Swedish wood arrived on a huge truck. There was the driver and two helpers with the truck, all of whom were Arabs; but it was not enough, so Soufiane quickly got hold of two more helpers who were Berbers, as a chibané (old man) I was not supposed to participate. The reading went like clockwork, so tea was subsequently brewed, which was consumed by everyone including me. When we sat on the wooden planks and drank the tea, it was strange to see the three Arabs sitting and talking together, and the other Berbers talking among themselves. When I subsequently asked Soufiane why they did not talk to the Arabs, he explained to me that it was too difficult to hold a conversation with them. The Berbers understood some of the Arabs' Dahia, but the Arabs understood just a little Tamazight. It gives some food for thought.

Despite the fact that I have just written that classical Arabic is also taught in schools, it is my experience that not very many people speak classical Arabic.

French is also compulsory in schools and many people speak French in Morocco, although not everyone speaks it. Incidentally, I maintain my French every day, as already written, via a language course on the Internet, since the French spoken in Morocco does not completely harmonize with correct French - a relic from the colonial era.

Oddly enough, I have noticed that suddenly there are more young people who speak English. When I first came to Morocco in 2012, almost no one spoke English; but now here in 2023 the picture is reversed. Many learn the language themselves with the help of their mobile phone and language courses on the Internet. If you ask the young people who mainly speak English why they learn it, the answer is always that it is the language spoken in the world, and it is also incredibly easy to learn.

Many Berbers have these signs

Painted on their door. It is Zeta, or as I have also heard it Zar in the Berber alphabet, (the Tifinagh alphabet). I have asked several people what the difference is in them; but received no response. I have also found that they use them randomly on the doors. They say it means free man, and the signs look pretty much like a human too. My brother-in-law claims that when it is painted on the door it means: Here live free people, here live Berbers!

Although we all know the red Moroccan flag with the green five-pointed star in the middle,

it is not the only flag in Morocco. The Berbers have their own flag, almost like the Scanians and Bornholmers have their own flag.

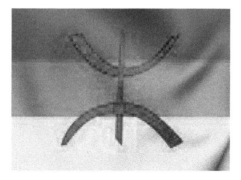

We already know the sign, the letter in the middle, it is Zeta in the Berber alphabet, tifinagh; (that's what free man means - Berber). The wide blue stripe at the top symbolizes Morocco's sea areas, the Mediterranean and the Atlantic. The green stripe in the middle symbolizes green Morocco, the Morocco you experience when you travel by train from Marrakech to the north, these are the large green fields you see when you approach Casablanca. The yellow stripe at the bottom symbolizes the yellow Morocco, the desert!

18

Population of Morocco

Since I always get tired of too many numbers, and I know many of you feel the same way, I will limit myself as much as possible with the numbers.

There are two large population groups and some minorities living in Morocco. The two major population groups are the Berbers and the Arabs. There are a total (2023) of just under 40 million inhabitants in Morocco, and it is estimated that approximately 40% of these are Berbers. It can be difficult to say exactly how many there are of each, as it is inevitable that Berbers and Arabs marry, and what about the children, are they Arabs or Berbers? It is a bit strange, as I said, I live my life in "Berber country" and have found in "this country" that if an Arab woman or an Arab man marries a Berber, their children are considered Berbers.

Mischievous as I am, I have not been able to keep my mouth shut; but I have learned, that it has not gone down well.

The Berbers are the population group that has inhabited Morocco the longest. They lived here when the Arabs made their inroads in the years (approximately) 700 to 1100. The Arabs gradually converted the Berbers to Islam. I don't know exactly what the Berbers believed in before then, but I have in special situations experienced reminiscences from an earlier religion with the use of incense and the burning of special herbs, even though prayers were prayed in the Muslim way. My thoughts often go back to the religion I experienced among the mountain Indians (Mayans) in Mexico, where Christianity and the indigenous religion were mixed together.

Many Berbers live in the mountains and desert areas; but my private theory is that they originally inhabited the whole of Morocco, but were displaced by the invading Arabs.

There is a world of difference between Berbers and Arabs. This applies to appearance, size, clothes, lifestyle and language.

19

When you see the little Berber women with their variegated, colorful clothes, shawls and scarves, you always know they are Berbers. The Arab women are usually larger and their clothes are much more uniform with a uniform color which is often black or dark.

The Berber men and the Arab men often wear similar clothes, both European and from the Middle East. If they are wearing Middle Eastern clothes, you can often trace a greater variation in colors and patterns in the Berber man's clothing. Also, the Berber man is usually smaller than the Arab man.

The Berbers are thrifty, friendly people who have lived in harmony with nature for many years, and this characterizes them to this day. They are quiet, but still love to gossip in their own way.

The population, which is for the most part Berbers in our village, are definitely not poor Berbers, it must be said that it is a village with relatively well-off residents; but still their mountain life clings to them. Many keep chickens and even goats and sheep, which they drive past our house every day. Yes, even my dear wife Jamila almost always has a couple of hens or a couple of roosters walking on our lower terrace - at the moment there is a rooster that disturbs my night's sleep; already at four in the morning he starts howling. There were actually two roosters that were crowing each other; so the otherwise patient neighbors quietly asked Jamila if she couldn't settle for a rooster. The end of it all was that the resident Hamid got the one cock for the soup pot, as Jamila would not eat her good cock!

In similar Arab cities you do not see this picture. I have also learned how the old nomadic culture still clings to the Berbers. For example, we have some neighbors who, in principle, live permanently in their house - but still don't. Sometimes they disappear over the other side of the mountains to grandma, where they help with the mountain farm – goats, sheep, turkeys and chickens, as well as a little oasis that they cultivate. Then suddenly after a month or a half they are back in their house again. I have asked Jamila how they are dealing with the children's school. Jamila replies that there are also schools over there, that they attend while they are with best.

Our neighbor Mohamed, who is a night watchman in Aourir, has just lived with his wife and three children in their unfinished house next to us for a month. Now they are back over on the other side of the mountain, so it is only Mohamed who sometimes sleeps in the house during the day.

The Berber family below my studio and workshop over on the other side of another mountain, have divided it up in such a way that when the wife's parents have to harvest their crops, the wife and children make a pilgrimage up to grandma and grandpa to actively participate in the harvest; it usually takes more than a month.

The Arabs, who have sat on much of the administration and held the major positions in trade and business, are more vocal and direct in their communications.

It must be said that in recent years a great change has taken place, so many Berbers have today been given large positions both in the public and in the private sector; but nevertheless the previously mentioned demonstrations took place in Rabat.

I can best illustrate the difference between Berbers and Arabs with the following little story: I once visited an Arab specialist. When I entered the waiting room or rather the waiting salon, it was decorated with fine paintings and other art. When I entered the doctor's office, the room was equally magnificent and the apparatus and instruments he had were of the latest date. I absolutely cannot complain about the treatment, it was top notch! That was the fee too – according to Moroccan conditions.The next time I visited a small Berber doctor. His waiting room was spartan with a simple picture of King Mohamed VI. When I came in to see him, he had the same apparatus and instruments as the Arab doctor, but of an older date. I absolutely cannot complain about his treatment either, it was also top notch, although his fee was less than half that of the Arab doctor.

I have experienced the same with dentists, where the Berber dentist's clinic was more spartan like the Berber doctor's; but the price, on the other hand, was also significantly lower. The repair of my teeth was reduced by several thousand dirhams (the currency in Morocco, 1 dirham = approx. 0.70 DKK) when I consulted the Berber dentist after getting a price proposal from the Arab dentist.

Then there is the whole discussion of the Taureges, the blue people, whose skin is also said to have been dyed blue by their blue clothes.

Some claim that the blue-clad people found in the Moroccan Sahara are not Tauregs, but Berbers. Others claim that it is only part of the population living towards Mali that are Tauregs and still others claim that true Tauregs are only found in Niger, Mali, southern Algeria and southern Libya and that there are only about one million left.

I have no idea what is right; but can tell you that our blue-clad here in our village, Hassan, who as a Taureg drives around with his camels at Tamraght beach and sells rides on the camels to tourists, is not a Taureg but a Berber. But don't tell anyone, the illusion should not be broken!

A few years ago I met a man, near Agadir, that was when we had the big drought. The man claimed to be a Taureg and lived in southern Morocco on the border with Mautania. I saw pictures from the area, and both his appearance and stories seemed credible. He told how, because of the drought, he had been forced to slaughter a large part of his wealth, the camels. He also said that the Tauregs, where he lived, spoke a Berber dialect.

My wife Jamila has a more practical division, Berbers, Arabs, French and the desert people. She has the French with her, as there are quite a lot French living in Morocco, and the desert people are pretty much the same, whether they are Berber or not.

You see it when you go by bus from Gare Routiere (the big bus station) in Agadir, where the desert people who go on the buses to Ourzazate and Zagora stand out from others because of their distinctive desert clothing.

A short time ago, when I was at a lecture in Denmark, I sat next to a woman who had been in a kibbutz in Israel in her young days with her now deceased husband. Before they went back to Denmark, they had made a detour to Morocco, where they had been on what we today call trekking. They had seen and experienced a lot in Morocco and also many "veiled women", so she asked a lot about the women in Morocco. How oppressed were they, and how did their husbands treat them?

I had to admit that many women wear headscarves in Morocco, both Berber women and Arab women; but at the same time I could tell her, that it is not a sign of oppression. I have learned in several both Berber and Arab families that it is the mother who sits on the cash register. At our local Wednesday market close to where I live in Hay Assersif, I strangely meet women who wear veils over their faces so that you can only see their eyes, usually I see very few of these women. It took a while before I found the explanation. When we buy in the market, it is not unusual for us to haggle a little about the price, so that a woman with her face covered can haggle all she wants about the price, without the seller knowing that it is "the rich Mohamed's" wife. At the dentist, who pulls out teeth and grinds them, as well as makes prostheses, you also see quite a few veiled women; but that again has its explanation. It's quite smart to cover your mouth with cloth when you're missing half of your teeth and waiting for the new denture.

So if you think that these are oppressed women, you have to think again. I have also experienced in the collective taxi that a woman with a covered face on her way to the market took a liking to me. She hit her own thighs and hit me on the thighs as she laughed and talked; when I got off before the souk (market) she was very upset; but I had to go home to Jamila.

There was also once a woman without her face covered, who was very interested in me in the public taxi. At the same time, she talked quite a bit with the taxi driver. When she got out of the taxi a little way before me, I got a loving pat on the cheek. When we drove again the driver told her that she had been left alone, and thought I might be a good partner for her, so he had promised to call her to let her know if I was available! I had to inform him, that I was married to Jamila.

Jamila loves to cast and brick; but since it is not well seen that women do this kind of work, she wraps herself in a large scarf when she works outside. She thinks that no one can recognize her, although anyone can see that it is the little troll at work.

Before we bought our current house, we lived in an Arab quarter nearer Agadir to the Atlantic Ocean. Some of the women here worked in the nearby fish oil factories and were very independent women who met several times a week after work "up on the mountain," where they discussed the day's events over a cup of coffee or tea.

My four sisters-in-law, whom I have gotten to know over the years, are absolutely not oppressed, although it can be difficult to compare a Danish and a Moroccan marriage.

Women drive cars as well as men, although there are still no female drivers on buses and taxis. But on the other hand, there are female soldiers, gendarmes and police officers in Morocco.

So there is the question of whether alcohol is drunk in Morocco? In the Morocco I came to 12 years ago, no one in my family or circle of friends drank alcohol, with the exception of a couple of my brothers-in-law who are fishermen. One managed to quit 5 years before he died. The other is still alive and hasn't had any alcohol in any form for 2 years now. I have to confess that I scared the wits out of him. For I have said that if he starts again, Allah will punish him very severely, it works! I have also told him, that if I can quit (just had my 10 year anniversary) so can he.

Yes, and then there was the time Jamila and I traveled to Rabat a few times. That was before we got married; Jamila had to get a visa for Sweden and we also had to get the marriage papers in order. Normally we traveled by bus from Agadir to Marrakech and then by train to Rabat. But when Jamila's brother Hassan explained that it was much easier to take the bus all the way, we jumped on it! It was much more troublesome and tiresome; we were stuck in Casablanca traffic for several hours and didn't arrive in Rabat until night.

We were lucky to be accommodated at "our hotel" close to the Gare de

Train (station); but there was no serving, tea or coffee to be had, so we went down the street, where there was a restaurant right next door. When we looked in through the windows, I couldn't believe my eyes, there was wine, singing, music and clinking of cups. There was beer, whiskey and booze on all the tables and on the bar counter. It reminded me of a Spanish bar. Jamila explained that it was very normal in this part of Morocco.

The result was that we did not go in; but instead would go to a coffee restaurant on the first floor, diagonally opposite.

Best as we wanted to go up the stairs to the restaurant we were held back by a police officer who refused us entry, there was a raid coming! We were ordered to go home to our hotel! So we ended up at the hotel and had to settle for drinking the mineral water we had in the bottle.

Alcohol sales in Morocco take place almost like in Australia from special bottle shops or, as in Sweden, from Systembolaget.

Travel, arrival and stay in Morocco

Today I left for Morocco, Sunday 13/8 2023. I was just supposed to have my first great grandchild's naming party yesterday Saturday 12/8 2023, before leaving today.

I have already told a little about how I travel. It is mostly with Ryanair. When I go to Copenhagen, the last several times I have traveled from Agadir to Milan, where I stopover at the new Bergamo airport. Here I waited for a few hours, after which I continued to Copenhagen Airport, Kastrup. All in all, it takes approx. 18 to 20 hours, from when I drive from my home and until I reach my apartment in Perstorp in Sweden or my caravan at Røsnæs near Kalundborg in Denmark. The trip can usually be done for an amount between DKK 700 and DKK 900. During holiday periods it can be DKK 1,100 to DKK 1,200.

When traveling back, it has been difficult to find a journey that ended in Agadir, so I have mostly traveled via the new Brandenburg airport outside of Berlin. Sometimes I have taken Flixbus from Ingerslevsgade, close to Copenhagen Central Station and directly to Brandenburg Airport, where I only walk 400 meters to enter the departure hall.

Other times I've taken easyJet; it's almost hip as hap in terms of money and time, and I avoid the long walk at Kastrup airport out to the low-cost terminal. The Ryanair flight I hop on in Berlin, Brandenburg flies to Marrakech, so the problem is that I sometimes have to spend the night there at "my little hotel El Kanarie," in order to take the bus the 250 km to Agadir the next day. It is not the large sums hotel and bus costs. An overnight stay on El Kanarie has gradually crept up to DKK 235 and the bus costs DKK 77; but that's all the time spent traveling, sometimes almost two days; it annoys me.

But this time I have tried something new, which I have knitted together myself, strangely enough the journey was not found on the search engine Momondo.

I was supposed to take off from Kastrup Airport at 14:00 today and land in Krakow, Poland at 15:35 but we left 15 minutes late and landed 15 minutes late as there were problems in the departure terminal, so we had to leave an extra trip.

In Krakow it was incredibly easy, I could stay inside the airport, which I am not used to in the other low-cost airports I frequent, even though they are new and completely modern. It has almost become normal for me to exit the arrivals terminal and then re-enter through security and the entire pier to the departures terminal. But here in Krakow, I just took the elevator up in the departure terminal and very quickly found the gate from which we were to fly, in the clear airport. I always check in in advance and travel with minimal hand luggage.

We landed 10 minutes early in Agadir, where it was like being in an oven. I was wearing my thermal jacket, which I didn't have room for in the backpack; so I had to keep it on as I had to have my hands free for immigration where we stood in line. Suddenly there was a vacant civil servant, whom I spontaneously went over to; he said: "Hey Poul,

26

welcome back, how are you?" I have no idea, if I know him, but my passport was stamped in record time! When I got to the person, who checks the luggage and how much money you have with you, he just waved me through. Just before you get all the way out of the airport, there were a couple of young people selling SIM cards for the phone, it's the first time I've seen it; but it must be said to be both a cheap and smart solution.

All in all I was out of Agadir airport in under 10 minutes.

My good friends Hassan and Aaziz, who were supposed to pick me up, hadn't arrived yet; but they came after less than 10 minutes.

Despite the late hour, at 11pm, everyone in Morocco stayed outside, so it was heavy traffic the 40km all the way home to Hay Assersif, where, to Jamila's great joy, I arrived early for once.

The joy of seeing each other was great, so even though I was very sore after the journey, I had to have some proper hugs and something to eat and drink.

Despite the heat I managed to sleep, I slept like a rock and did not wake up until breakfast at 9 o'clock the next morning and was a little surprised when I saw the already mentioned 2 roosters strutting on the terrace. I had to state once again, that Jamila is and will be a Berber girl.

Because of my schooling, I am the one who is connected to the various authorities and therefore pays electricity and water etc. I am also the one who makes the big purchases for the same reason. If I have Jamila with me, I get distracted by the seller's recommendations and back-talk, so I do the shopping alone.

So after breakfast I put the big backpack on my back and went down the mountain, where I just waited 3 minutes before an aktaf (collective taxi) came and picked me up.

It's a mixed crowd that runs these acts, some are gorgeous, nice people and a few are scoundrels. I have therefore had to respect myself three times, when I have given them a fist on the shoulder and threatened with the ribs; it helped! Two of them came "creeping" the next day and the third pulled over to the side of the road when, three weeks later, I was walking down the street and asked, if I wanted to ride along. All three are today my friends!

It's talk all the time, mixed French and Tamazight and dahia, I write it as we say it, so it's probably not grammatically correct. "Salam, ça va, beher!" says the taxi driver. I reply: "Alhamdulillah!" All the while we start to roll off. "Je n'ai pas vu toi beaucoup de temps, pourquoi?" continues the driver. "C'est parce que j'étais au Danemark!" I continue. Then I say: "Safe!" That means stop, because we've just reached my friend Soufiane's timber shop, I have to go in and say: "Hello!" for him.

28

However, it didn't turn into so much philosophical talk today, because there were customers in the shop, so I continued over to the lady, where I wanted to pay the electricity bill; but I was not allowed to; it was too small; I could pay it all next time.

I continued walking the few kilometers that are down through Aourir, past the hardware stores, past a single bank, past the bread sellers, the baker, the fishmongers, the restaurants that grill the fish you buy from the fishmongers, and reached the spice shop which also has oatmeal in bulk. Here I was also asked about where I had been, and what I had done.

Then I was at the dentist further down the street; there were still 10 days of holiday, so I have to wait to repair my teeth.

After that I passed by the big pharmacy, where luckily the pharmacist didn't see me; I saved time there!

The tour continued down through the arcade with all the butcher shops, where the butchers can't help but hang the hindquarters out in front of the shop, even though it was banned during the corona crisis. Most of them even had a counter made of glass in front of the shop, so that hygiene was more under control. But as Jamila says: "You should always check that the meat doesn't smell before you buy it!"

I wasn't supposed to have meat today, but chickens, which are bought freshly slaughtered. It could wait, the café attracted me, it is set back to the main coastal road that connects Agadir with Essaouira and passes the immediate baths and surf areas of Tamraght and Targazout. Further on there are even more such areas. The beach at Aourir has gradually also become a sought-after bathing and surfing area.

At "my old cafe Inou," there was a great life, eating breakfast and drinking tea and coffee. There was more shouting than usual; there were tourists, Arab and French, so I sat quietly, a little back in the café. Fortunately, it was the calm bartender Hassan who was there today. He also wanted to know what I had been doing and where I had been; but we managed it fairly quickly so I could have my new tea.

When I see all the tourists queuing at the bank next door to the cafe and hear them discussing and talking with their relatives sitting in the cafe outside, I often think of myself when I was a tourist traveling around the world with my family.

I drank the tea and greeted a few acquaintances, paid 10 dirhams (7 DKK), the 2 dirhams were tips and went back to the shopping street, where I bought the chickens, vegetables and a whole lot of other things.

However, I had to walk up the street a bit before I could jump on an aktaf again. It's an incredible play that's going on. The gendarmes, who make sure, that everything goes right, also have to reject the act victims, so if there are gendarmes at the end of the street, the act victims stay a little further up.

It is very normal that if a person is caught driving speed exit, he gets a, seen from our eyes, smaller fine and loses the right to drive the car for four days.

The authorities have to close their eyes to keep the infrastructure together.

Since I couldn't bear to drag all my shopping up the mountain to our house, I had the driver drive all the way to the house, which I usually pay 10 dirhams for.

On Tuesday I went to Aourir again, though there was not much to buy; but the café pulled.

Although Aourir is a trading town with a large catchment area, a huge market is held every Wednesday - the souk close to where we live, so on Wednesday I had to go to the souk to buy cheaply for the whole

coming week.

I already started walking down the mountain at 10 o'clock in only 24 degree heat with my empty backpack and large shopping trolley. I reached the souk after just 5 minutes. As you can see in the pictures, most had managed to set up their stalls, while some had chosen to present their goods on the ground.

I noticed at once, that there were few tourists, no Arabs or French; they probably preferred the beach today. But there were quite a few women with wide behinds who pushed themselves forward.

The boys were busy driving goods for all those who could not transport everything they had bought themselves.

31

Hassan is an old acquaintance; that's him in the picture. He helps Mustafa sell vegetables. Hassan always services me, I don't save any money, but now it's very nice. I bought various oriental vegetables including potatoes and basal. Basal is onion in Arabic and the word is easy to remember, because onion is the basic thing in all our cooking.

The vegetables had actually increased a bit while I've been in Denmark and Sweden, so I wonder how the fruit was? The apples, pretty red-cheeked apples, cost converted DKK 5.60/kg and the grapes cost DKK 10.50/kg, so there was a bit of each in the sack.

I also had roasted peanuts, natural candy, cookies and raisins on the shopping list, which I bought from the usual little Berber man who always salutes me! I always remember to say hello back! He is good to deal with, because you never get too little, on the contrary, he has a "patience" weight, unlike others who have forgotten what is written in the Koran - guessed right - it says that you must not cheat on the scales!

The boy who helps his father sell olives got 10 dirhams stuck in his hand, after which I got my usual bag of pink olives, which in my old days I have come to love so much.

The picture shows one of the merchants' range of goods. I usually only shop at the same one.

I do this because he is cheap and quick to calculate correctly, without us having to discuss. So it turned out to be 12 rolls of toilet paper, 2 bottles of washing-up liquid, 4 kg of washing powder, 2 pcs. liquid hand soap, 2 pcs. regular hand soap and ¾ liter hair shampoo. I paid him DKK 69.60 for the entire mole.

Before I went home I also needed 15 eggs, normally I buy 30 eggs but I bought 15 eggs yesterday in Aourir because Jamila didn't have any more left.

Home with it all

calculated that I would have to buy 20 pieces. boards of 4.50 m.

It was getting to be evening and we sat down on our lower roof terrace. It was one of those peaceful evenings where we could sit and watch thFortunately, the temperature had only risen to 29 degrees, so it was just bearable so I could get some work done.

I promised Jamila before I went to Denmark and Sweden that I would make a new sofa arrangement when I came back. It's not because there's anything wrong with the old; but I feel totally honored, she prefers my raw 1001 nights style so I better get going. When I finish the sofas, Jamila's sister Habiba will have the old ones.

I made drawings, measured and messed and reacted in the afternoon. When the drawings were approved by Jamila, I calculated that IFortunately, the temperature had only risen to 29 degrees, so it was just bearable so I could get some work done.

would have to buy 20 pieces. boards of 4.50 m.of terrace. It was one of those peaceful evenings where we could sit and watch thFortunately, the temperature had only risen to 29 degrees, so it was just bearable so I could get some work done.

e opposite side of the valley with its mountaine opposite side of the valley with its mountain conjuncture and of course the women and men sitting on the mountain looking over to our side of the valley. The sunset and the light were amazing with reds, yellows and emerald greens all while the sun was setting.

Where we lived before, out by the Atlantic Ocean, both women and men sat in the same way on the quiet, peaceful evenings. But it wasn't the mountains they were looking at, it was the sea and the sun that finally sank into the sea.

Of course, it took some time before we found the "sweating boxes" where we tried to sleep.Jamila is always up early; I would like to lie a quarter of an hour longer, she get the coffee and oatmeal ready. Today was no exception.

However, I quickly got it all sorted out, as I only had the three new sofas in mind, so I was down at Soufiane's a little after 10 o'clock, where I ordered and paid for the 20 boards, as well as paid for our mutual friend Rachid to transport the boards home on his little mini truck. I continued down to the cafe where I am sitting now.

Just read a post on Facebook about a man in Denmark who had sat on the train tracks and was just waiting for the train to come and end his life. The writer of the notice succeeded in getting the train to stop 7 meters before the man reached it. Subsequently, the two talked together on a bench, where the unhappy suicide candidate explained that he had nothing to live for. He was a drug addict, mentally ill, had begged for help, but there was no help to be had; no one would help him, and he had no friends.

I immediately thought about what makes some societies, such as ours here in Morocco, accept these kinds of people to a greater degree. To that extent, there is room and acceptance for people with special behavior. Some work as parking attendants, some as helpers at the fishmonger etc.

Although I have thought a lot about what the reason is, I cannot find a single answer. Maybe religion, maybe the climate with more outdoor life, maybe a gene that the people here have to a greater extent than the people up in Denmark, or perhaps the fact that Moroccan society, as far as earnings and spending on luxury items are concerned, is very different with less money available to the individual, so the tolerance for it each individual becomes larger. Unfortunately, I have found that the tolerance for others who think differently in today's Denmark is becoming less and less!

I know this is wishful thinking; but if we in Denmark actively change our attitude and allow more of these fellow human beings into our society and into our families, we kill two birds with one stone, we avoid:

1. that more of our fellow human beings do not need to see a psychiatrist or psychologist.

2. reduced waiting lists.

Unfortunately, I think it requires a huge self-awareness and effort by everyone from the individual, the authorities and the government; and whether it is possible in the present situation, I do not know.

What happened on the way home? I got a confirmation of my just thought thoughts!

Just as I stepped out of the café, a large, black car pulled up on the side of me and the side window was rolled down. Inside the windows sat a well-to-do Arab family in the air-conditioned car. At first I thought they would ask for directions; but no; the family man sitting at the wheel and doing the talking just wanted to know why I was wearing fuchia (summer dress)? I promptly replied a little sternly: "Big fat, old man and very hot!" They all understood it, laughed loudly and drove on. I don't think the same thing happened in Denmark.

Right after I met my sister-in-law Essaddia in a small square; I didn't miss kisses and hugs, I even got a smack right in the middle of the mouth. It did not seem to me now that I had been away so long; but I must have been! No one took notice of our hugging, the wide tolerance is worth noting!

Rachid didn't come with the boards until 6 p.m., so we got them stowed on the ground floor so I can start my sofa work.

I found this morning that my saw and other tools are in my combined studio and workshop in another small village, Hafsi behind a mountain further out towards the Atlantic, so after Jamila had given me a haircut I headed back down our mountain and discovered that none other than the taxi driver Said was sitting waiting for customers. He has sailed with Spanish fishing trawlers, so there is always a bit of rubbish Spanish to be spoken! Said lives in Hafsi himself, so he knows exactly how to drive me over the mountains to my workshop. He charges 20 dirhams/14DKK to drive me directly to the door.

Picture from the trip over the mountains.

Here is a small random selection of pictures from the apartmenr/workshop, as well as the tool I picked up.

Workshop/atalier requires an explanation. For approx. 3 years ago I realized, that I needed more space for all my tools and painting supplies. I also needed peace for my work, so I searched with light and lantern for a workspace. I found it via my good friend Hassan in Hafsi up on the mountainside above his apartment. I had to pay the famous sum of 700 DKK in rent per month. When I had arrived with all my things and had put them in place, I discovered that there were 2 empty rooms and a small toilet, like ours, as well as a shower. "Who lives here and how do we arrange it with them when I come." I asked. Hassan explained that they also belonged to me; they were in on the deal! So what did I do? I bought boards like now and made 2 sofas, a table a kitchen cabinet, a desk, a large, combined living room and wardrobe and finally a bed. So now I have an apartment where I can stay once in a while, work with my tools, paint a little and write what I want. The roof also belongs to the apartment; I installed electricity up there; there was already water, so now Naïma, Hassan's wife, can wash and hang the clothes to dry.

I probably don't know how much I'll get done today, because the temperature is currently 37 degrees and expected to rise to 41 degrees!

I lay on the couch until almost 4 p.m., then went downstairs and started sawing the boards into pieces. Carried all up to the second floor and installed it.

During the project, sister Essaddia came with her daughter Mariam. Although I was drenched in sweat and probably didn't smell very good, I was going to have the same trip again, believe it or not. I had thought that both Jamila, Essaddia, and Mariam had gone into the salon downstairs; but they stayed; it was interesting to watch me work and they helped me a little. I finished the first sofa. You will probably get to see it; but I think we'll wait until the other two are ready and I might have acquired cushions.

Essaddia had couscous with the cow stomach, which tastes really good, even though they are not on the menu at home in Denmark. We don't get them that often, as Jamila is "too Danish" and doesn't like them.

The following day, despite a hot afternoon, I managed to fabricate one more sofa. When I finished it I announced that I would be "taking a vacation" the next day.

It didn't turn out to be much of a holiday, because I had planned to order cushions and matelas, which usually takes a little time, as I have to get them at the right price. The ones we have now were quite expensive due to the fact, that they are made of molded rubber, which was the alpha and omega a few years ago. But they have the flaw that if you lie on them too much, they become deformed. So we go back to the classic ones which are mostly kapok.

I had calculated a bit and figured about 1200 dirhams. I remembered to put on my Berber garb and have a bit of a long beard when I left this morning.

The vast majority of times I have dealt with Abdullah. He is not as old as he looks; he is probably no more than his mid-forties, although somehow he has the appearance and features of an older man. He has a little trouble understanding the "machine drawings" I make, so I have to "cut it all out of cardboard" for him!

But after some back-and-forth, he came up with a total price for the three matelas of 900 dirhams, while saying, "I don't want to negotiate with you today, we've known each other so long that we're dropping the show! " Knowing that the price was extremely favorable, we set to work. It was promised to be finished in two days; but as always I calculate three days. He got 400 dirhams out of the 900 dirhams as a deposit, advance; it is I who decide it; everything is written down on a small note that I keep in my pocket.

On the way home I have to remember to buy another pack of 4 mm wood screws for the last sofa. The screws cost 25 dirhams, approximately 25 SVK. In Sweden, where I have bought all that kind of stuff over the last 15 years, I have to pay 100 SVK for a package of the same size! I often wonder who runs with the big profits.

Later, when we've got the cushions in place, I'll buy covers. It also requires negotiation, but now let's see if Abdullah doesn't have a good price for them as well.

The following day I stayed home to make the third couch. I took it easy; the salon is not right-angled, so I made the sofa to fit exactly in the corner; it was therefore only finished in the afternoon.

After that I wanted to do laundry. I do some of our laundry because I know how to get the soap out of the clothes. Sometimes when Jamila has washed the clothes there are soap residues in them, and then I protest. I should rather say that the washing machine we have is one with a tub with a rotor at one end and a centrifuge at the other end.

41

This is what the washing machine looks like from above, many of these machines are made in Turkey

We have had automatic washing machines in Sweden without success, as Jamila often chooses a wrong programme, so this one works, even if sister Habiba were to come by to wash.

Many Berbers in the mountains still wash in the streams. Several times I have seen the women stand with their bums in the air and give the clothes a good shake, rinse them and hang them to dry on the usually prickly bushes.

The funniest and most inventive washing machine I have seen was on the outskirts of Tamraght, where a woman washed in an old oil drum. That requires an explanation! A board with a hole in the middle was strung over the oil barrel, which was of course cleaned and free of oil. In this hole was fitted a shaft with a whisk at the bottom of the barrel and a handle at the top of the barrel. So as the woman turned the handle, the clothes were washed.

I hung the laundry to dry on the top roof, sat in the chair and looked at the mountains, I saw clouds coming into the valley from the south, but thought nothing more of it. The temperature was comfortable, probably between 25 degrees and 30 degrees. After ½ hour I felt the clothes, they were almost dry, so I went downstairs, drank mint tea and talked to Jamila a bit.

When an hour had passed, I went up to get the dry clothes. But it was wet and the bottom of the laundry basket was full of water. The clouds I had seen had produced a short but heavy shower of rain! It's Morocco!

I didn't want to take the chance and leave the clothes hanging on the roof overnight, so I carried them all downstairs and hung them to dry inside the house.

It didn't turn into more rain, although I could see in the darkness that it had started to get foggy down in the valley. So I fetched another cup of tea and settled down on the lower terrace to enjoy the evening breeze and look at the crescent moon while thinking about the orange fireball and all the other strange celestial phenomena I had experienced in my life.

Oops! Now what was that? At one time, when I looked up at the sky, there were 28 lightnings or maybe 30 little white lights marching in one row, I had a hard time counting them, it flickered before my eyes. I summoned Jamila, who wanted to photograph them; but firstly, it wouldn't have been possible with the phone and secondly, they would have been gone when she got back.

Jamila had to know what it was? When I said I didn't know, she said I knew everything, so she didn't believe me. So the man who knows everything had to find an explanation. It succeeded, it must have been the rich man Elon Musk, who had sent up a new batch of satellites, which along the way were to be distributed to special positions, from which they were to function as telecommunications and internet satellites. I could feel myself believing the explanation.

I saw a few days ago on the mountain road from Assersif to Hafsi that there was an overturned, demolished house and have since wondered why?

Today, when Rachid drove the sofa cushions home, I got the explanation. The municipality has begun to demolish all non-legally built housing without mercy, so that we are approaching European and Danish standards and conditions. It is both good and bad! Now there will be less space for the odd existences! Some of the houses were very distinctive gems built by hippies during Morocco's hippie period. I am sure that in a few years, when history is written, the action will be regretted; but what happened is what happened!

It's not just here, but everywhere in the world, there's this rush to erase the hippie culture, and I ask myself, "Why?" Although the hippies were not constructive in many areas and did not fit into society, I believe that they had many values that we miss today.

Yesterday Wednesday I was once again at the Wednesday market; the shopping cart and backpack were a bit lighter this time as I had bought the basics last time.

After a coffee break at home with some of the good cookies I had bought, I hit the road one more time. This time it was Abdullah's turn, who had the mattress pads ready.

I quickly arranged the transport of them home. I immediately went over to Soufiane, where Rachid (the one with the little truck) was sitting enjoying life. I brought three more boards as Jamila and sister Habiba have a project, a plan that I have almost agreed to.

Jamila and I quickly put the matress in place, so now we just need to buy some covers and put them on. Jamila also has to sand and paint the wood; but it is somewhat unknown when that will be. It could be today, tomorrow or in a month. I'm not saying anything, it's not worth the discussion.

But here, as promised, is the preliminary result.

Late in the afternoon older sister Fatima and her son Eisa came. The daughter, whose name I can never remember, had stayed at home because of the heat.

Fatima makes a lot of noise and Eisa says nothing at all; he is about 14 years old and can hardly speak, no one knows why? He is a handsome, neat and friendly young man who is mentally deviant.

Fatima was married to Mohamed, whom I mentioned earlier. He was the one who managed to stop drinking alcohol 5 years before he died. He was a retired fisherman and earned a little extra by snorkeling for clams and squid. But 1 ½ years ago he drifted ashore lifeless. It was soon ascertained that he had not drowned; but that the heart had "gone out!" His doctor knew very well that he had a bad heart, but Mohamed had never told anyone, not even at home.

The house on the slope in Tamraght in which they lived belonged to Mohamed. But Mohamed's family let Fatima and the children stay. There is a small extra house belonging to the big house, which Fatima was given the right to dispose of, so that she can rent it out and thus earn an extra shilling to live on.

After Mohamed's death, I had to make a sofa for the family, so there was one more bed. The old sofa was to be used in the rental house.

I have told Jamila that of course we must help them. But they don't get any money, just like the rest of the family doesn't get any money either. They simply melt between their fingers in the heat. So when we had drunk, eaten and talked a bit, Fatima had the shopping bag she had brought loaded.

When I was on the toilet in the evening, I sat looking at a scorpion and it looked back at me. Jamila is an excellent scorpion and snake killer, so I shouted, "Jamila c'est un petit scorpion ici!" Immediately, in no time, Jamila was there and I heard the crunching sound of the scorpion being killed. Fortunately, I have never been bitten; but Jamila has been unlucky a few times. It takes a while for her, she gets sick for a day, but quickly recovers.

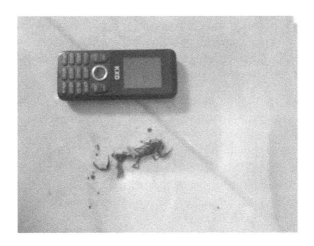

She didn't kill the scorpion with the cell phone; it's just there to show the aspect ratio.

Fortunately, the scorpions, like the small, black snakes, only come in when it gets warm; but the strange thing is that we can find them on all floors; why we never found out.

The cockroaches are there all the time, sometimes we have to make an extra effort to regulate the population; but they are sort of very peaceful; I know them in advance from my sailing in the tropics.

The geckos come in periods, right now we don't have any visible, even though it's very hot. But they are protected! I once learned in the East that if you kill a gecko, it means 1000 years of misfortune, where this myth comes from, I don't know!

Today, Thursday, I finally managed to get to an open door at the dentist. Only "la fille," the maid, was there; at home in Denmark she is called the clinic assistant.

She finds it difficult to smile and is a very reserved type. I have found that she lives at the clinic and has a room in the back; I guess it's part of her salary.

After she had looked at the tooth damage, I was shown the bench in the waiting room. After a quarter of an hour I heard it breathing on the stairs; I knew the breath, it was none other than Mama dentist who arrived.

I was immediately called in to see her, where I explained that I had chewed on an apple, so that the front teeth were broken from the prosthesis. So I had to have a hard time, and I knew that: "When you have a prosthesis, you don't chop an apple into yourself, you cut it into neat little pieces, that you eat." I bowed my head so she knew I was sorry I had ruined her masterpiece; it helped, she smiled and said, "Don't take it so hard, we can easily repair your prosthesis, come on Monday morning, then it's ready!"

Although I have just lamented the decline of hippie culture, I still sometimes meet old hippies when I travel the world. For some reason they often approach me even though I'm not a hippie. I myself believe that it is because I am an old man, where the smile is not far away; and probably also because I behave without coercion and naturally and try to treat everyone equally, as well as that I wear the clothes I want here and now; all these factors fit into the hippie pattern! What I like about hippies is that everyone is treated equally; everyone is worth the same despite their origin, skin color or religion. High-flying politics do not belong to hippies.

When I was sitting in the cafe a few hours ago and consulted my mobile phone, I saw that there were 4 hippies sitting outside in their colorful clothes. There were 3 elderly women and an elderly man, you were busy discussing something?

The man, who had a mild appearance, was probably in his 70s. Despite his age, he was a slender man. He had radiant blue eyes and the smile in his big long wild beard was unmistakable. It was a real hippie with his hair in a bun at the back of her neck.

When he got up, he headed towards me in the restaurant. He sat down opposite me and looked at me intently, then said in English: "I see; you are almost one of us! So now you have to listen here, the government has started demolishing houses that are not legally built, and how many of our houses in Paradise Valley do you think are listed? None! So it's a disaster for us, nothing more!" I knew Paradise Valley well, have been there and daily see people making pilgrimages there from my terrace in Hay Assersif.

"I know only too well, I've already seen houses fall!" I said.

He soon after told that he was born in Scotland, from where he had traveled the world early in his youth, first just as an ordinary traveler and later as a hippie. His name was Eric.

He had spent the last many, many years in Morocco, in Paradise Valley. He explained loudly that he had no intention of coming home to Scotland, he would just go even madder in the head than he already was!

When we had talked a little more, he held out a piece of paper and asked me if I dared to put my signature on it. I read it carefully. It was a protest document against the indiscriminate demolition of the houses. Before the demolitions, it had to be assessed whether the houses were somehow worthy of preservation for cultural and historical reasons. I guess no big deal could happen if I put my signature on the paper, so I did!

"I knew it, you're one of our kind; I saw it right away!" He continued. I did not comment on his statement; but just hummed.

I thought the session was over here; but had to believe because without further conversation Eric proclaimed out of thin air: "Homo Sapiens, you are a herd animal, always looking for a leader, you must have something to believe in and something to fear! You were made that way! A severe punishing God, a climate crisis because you have abused the values of the earth, nuclear power plants that spread death and destruction, the war that will be the last etc. You fall on your butt for a nod or a statement from a noble habit or a white coat at the right age .If anyone is so stupid as to oppose the official faith, they must be punished! It is the ruler and his people who have the right! That is the law of nature!

49

Yet there are outsiders, some Homo Sapiens, upright self-thinking people who cannot bear to follow suit, they think for themselves, many of them are old with their intellect intact. They are perhaps the worst at resisting, because they have seen and experienced your H. C. Andersen's 'The Emperor's New Clothes' several times in their lives. They have seen history repeat itself again and again, so their belief in authority towards those in power is no longer present.

They don't jump on the glue stick anymore, on the contrary!

Now we're sort of at the heart of the matter! That is why various people in power fear the statement of old scientists and all the rest of us thoughtful old people. Do we even have a climate crisis. In the late 1970s we also had a climate crisis; then we feared a new ice age! But it was cancelled!" Eric was about to take a sip of the mint tea Hassan had provided, so I took the opportunity to thank him many times for his input. He had understood that I understood his message, so he said no more. I didn't escape some huge, powerful hippie hugs before he sat down laughing to the ladies.

Suddenly, when I looked up from my cell phone, the black grinning hippie beard was sitting across from me again. I thought I got rid of Eric! But had to believe! He had more on his mind, he had more to proclaim: "Europe you meet your doom with the sticky web of regulations, certificates on everything and everyone, rules and norms you have entangled yourself in. You will suffocate in a an impenetrable web. A web that inhibits all reasonable action! Believe me, there is a difference between machines and people!" I nodded and hummed, which he was very pleased with, so after a few more heavy pats on my old sore shoulders, I was invited out to them in Paradise Valley. I probably haven't visited them out there yet.

I knew that what Eric was talking about could easily be true, because I know and sometimes talk to old scientists who have divergent views and opinions about the climate. They write one post after another to the news media; but being slowed down?! The only one that delivers the posts in Denmark is Jyllands Posten! It's great that there are still media that have objective journalism!

As for Europe, I had recently heard many similar statements, and Eric's was not the last.

I suddenly imagined how, as a boy, I was sitting out in the kitchen at my father and mother's house when they had a party and my brother Henning and I were not allowed to join.

Officer Nielsen, our resident, who was the long arm of the law, was also considered a wise man, so everyone listened to him devoutly when he explained that there would never be another war in this world, especially my mother listened, because she feared the war. Officer Nielsen explained that they had founded an international organization, the United Nations, so instead of fighting, they could now talk things out in a matter-of-fact manner.

The trees have never grown into the sky! The UN stretched its legs for itself in several ways. A whole book could be written about what went wrong; it will be far too extensive to bring it here.

The reality was, despite Officer Nielsen's words, that one war followed in the wake of the other. Although I am not a politician by any means, I believe that we have been too blue-eyed in our belief in the UN as the righteous big brother. I clearly confess that I am skeptical of the organization's dispositions and even regard some as hoof solutions.

This applies not least to the UN climate panel IPCC, which in my opinion lacks objectivity. Only people with the same opinion and attitude are allowed in. A bit of backlash would have been in order, especially when advising an entire world, its governments and other organizations. It is sad, because the IPCC should be for everyone, have breadth and depth and not just have a narrow inner circle of advisers with similar views, so I am tempted to conclude that if the other departments and panels of the UN function in the same way, it hurts a great deal of doubt about the UN's overall dispositions, recommendations and measures.

As I said, the hippie culture has many good sides that have helped to change our square world, I admit that clearly. The negative side of the culture is of course the abuse, both with hash, other drugs and alcohol, which I sincerely hope the new hippies, because there will always be hippies in this world, will reduce over time. But unfortunately the problem is not just the hippies; it is a problem in all peoples and cultures of the world to a greater or lesser extent. It is sad that we let these drugs dominate our lives. But I'm not the right person to comment on that.

Regarding the demolition of illegally built houses, I have previously explained that it is part of a huge government's planning for a more uniform, cleaner and more attractive Morocco. Huge, huge work has been and is being done to achieve this. What I am aware of and register is naturally in my surroundings; that is, in Agadir with surroundings and the other neighboring towns, including "our" Aourir.

Patch solutions are not carried out here, as I so often see in Denmark due to savings, most recently with the sewerage on Lundevej in Kalundborg, where our old house is located, instead of the promised sewerage replacement, a sock is now just pulled inside the sewer pipe.

Well, in Morocco it takes place in a completely different, overall way! The whole road is being broken up, old sewer pipes and electric cables are being removed, new ones are being laid and installed, new ballast in the road, new different roadway, many places with rambla, as in Barcelona and new wide pavements, often with nice new plantings both on the rambla and by the sidewalk.

Once again, if King Mohamed VI can keep Morocco together, which I sincerely hope, as I wrote before, it will be the country of tomorrow, and it will also be with a high level of education.

I saw the same pattern in Japan in the late 1960s, and then predicted Japan's growth (which, unfortunately, has changed in recent years). Now I predict Morocco's future growth in the same way. Here is initiative, courage and skill. It's a fantastic development Morocco has gone through just in the 11 years I've lived here.

I'd better get home; the temperature has crept up to 46 degrees, so I need an afternoon nap.

I didn't get much sleep in the heat; but lay thinking as I relaxed.

When you are a tourist and have bought a trip for a week, a fortnight or perhaps for three weeks; whether you have bought it as a charter trip or composed it yourself and arrive at a destination where the temperature touches 50 degrees or maybe even higher, in many cases you can lie and laze by the beach or by the hotel pool with your feet in the water and cool off the way. There is also air conditioning in many of the hotels. The excursions in nature and to sights can be strenuous and very hot; but they usually limit themselves to only one, two days at the most.

If, like me, you live in the heat for a long period without frequent beach visits and have daily things to deal with, the situation is different, we also don't have air conditioning, so inside the concrete house the temperature can be considerable.

Almost many years ago, long before I came to Morocco, I discovered the summer djellaba, which in Morocco we call fuchia (as opposed to the thick and warm one worn in winter, called sleeva). I then bought a summer djellaba in Egypt and although I was laughed at by my traveling companions, I discovered how comfortable it was to wear in the heat. It gave air to the nobler parts, so I avoided redness, irritation and skinlessness. It was easy to throw in a bucket of water in the evening, wring out and hang to dry, so it was ready for reuse the next morning. So, as I have previously written, I wear fuchia here in Morocco when the sun bakes and warms the country. It also has the advantage of limiting the sun's rays.

I had, yes I write had a quite excellent white fuchsia, which I sleep with in the heat without any kind of blanket or anything else over me. But last night when I was supposed to wear it, it was gone?! I knew it was Jamila who had removed it; but she would not go to confession. However, I know her Berber superstitions! The fuchsia was an heirloom from my late brother-in-law Abdullah, who died before I came "into the picture." I had been given it and one more, which also mysteriously disappeared, from sister Essaddia. .

Here you see the fuchsia I put on this morning!

I sat down quietly, drank some tea and thought; then I said to Jamila, "You have removed it because it belonged to Abdullah, who is dead, so you are afraid that I will die if I wear it, even though it has been washed countless times; isn't it right!" She readily admitted, so I didn't mind complaining, it was my fault she had removed it, so when I went to the cafe today I passed the tailor, who hadn't opened yet, so I ended up at the "cloth merchant " Ibrahim, who sells surplus goods from the garment factories up north in Morocco; some may have a small error. I made a deal with him. I got two new fuchias for 250 dirhams, equivalent to 175 DKK; if I had bought them in Agadir, it would have been more than double.

During my time sailing in the tropics, on a ship without air conditioning and working in a scorching machine, I learned to swallow two salt pills every day to supplement the salt I sweated out. The two pills meant that the salt balance was quite fine. But then one day the pills wore off! We couldn't get more for now. Just two days passed, then the cramps and discomfort started, it wasn't just me who felt like this. I instinctively salted the food extra, but it didn't really help. Then we reached

Bangkok, and suddenly at a bar I saw one of the girls measure out some salt on the teaspoon, pour it into a glass of water and drink it. I went over to her and asked how much and how often she did it and got a nice instruction. Subsequently, when I'm "in the heat" I've always followed her advice, and that's exactly what I'm doing now, so I avoid cramps and discomfort. Jamila complains that too much salt is not healthy.

Also, I always have a bottle of water with me in my backpack. When we talk about water, water is not just water. Much of the water found in homes in the world today is surface water that has been treated, conditioned. The water we have in Hay Assersif is no exception either. It is not conditioned with a chlorine compound; but with trisodium phosphate, so from a purely bacterial point of view it is possible to drink it, and many can drink it; but I can't drink it for long: I get pimples on my back from drinking it. It's okay to boil it for tea and coffee, then the chemical evaporates.

The next day, on the way home from Aourir in the evening, a gendarme suddenly stood by the curb and beckoned us in. Who were we, and where were we going? For once I hardly got to say anything; the driver was quick and said, "It is my old friend whom I have promised to drive home to Hay Assersif!" The gendarme looked a second time. I don't really think he believed it; but still he said, "Now drive him properly!" It is the first time I have experienced that we got free, even though we had entered the net. We didn't even have to show ID. I think it meant something, that the gendarme was alone.

Today, in the morning we drove for a garbage truck. The garbage trucks are very different here than in Denmark. It is a truck with a large bed with a lot of fiber sacks. Including the driver, there are five men on the wagon, and this has its own explanation, because unlike in Denmark, where everyone neatly sorts the waste and puts it in the correct compartments in the container, there is no one here who sorts the waste, all waste (usually not organic) are placed in the same barrel.

As the waste is collected by the four men, the same men begin to sort it into various sacks on the truck. It is a system that requires several hands; but it may not even be that bad when you take into account the higher unemployment in Morocco. The renovation system has almost reached us in the mountains; we paid, but we were let down, so we look at the time a bit.

I've had to have honey for the last few days, it's liquid honey that the bees have made from orange blossoms, it tastes really good and it's cheap if you buy it in the right places. I know an old honey seller, Hassan as my supplier is called, he sits on a small square in Aourir, from where he sells his products. Today he had had honey again, so after a lengthy greeting, I bought a glass for DKK 21.

It is Hassan You see in the following picture, in addition to honey he also sells amlou and other exotic sweet products. Amlou is powdered peanuts mixed with either olive oil or coconut oil, the amlou with the coconut oil is the cheap one. I almost think this version tastes the best. It tastes almost like our Nutella.

I also passed by the fish market, which gives our Danish fish markets the rear wheels. There are many vendors and a variety of fish.

Hassan is a wonderful person.

I immediately saw that my little friend Ahmed was there today. He is a small Berber man in his late twenties, he is not always there, only when he has fish to sell, he belongs to the lower rank among the sellers and only gets fish from the fishermen, when the supply is large; but he is my friend, always happy and welcoming with a big smile. He also never overcharges or cheats on the scale; on the contrary, I often get one more fish than I should have had.

I got a kilogram of sardines for DKK 8.40 and a baby tuna for DKK 17.50.

Here is the "catch of the day."

Every time I see a baby tuna, I think of my stays on the Venezuelan island Isla Margarita, where I once between Isla Margarita and los Frailes islands pulled 19 baby tuna up to sea in 1/2 hour helped by a little 12-year-old boy . But that is a completely different story.

Saturday I would stay at home. That is, I would not stay at home entirely; i would go down the mountain to get gas on a little home built cart i made from an old shopping bag cart. I didn't have to walk that far just a little kilometer to our local grocery store Hassan. I also had to have the day's ration of bread and various drinks.

Merchant Hassan was not there, it was Mustafa who was in the shop. Mustafa is a young man who has helped Hassan for many years. However, Mustafa has failed Hassan for the past few years, when he has attended the hotel and restaurant school in Agadir. Mustafa told me, that he had finished his education, so I wished him a hearty congratulations.

When we talked about, where he was going to work, he told me that he didn't want to work in Morocco. To my astonishment, he had applied for several jobs in the Arab world. He didn't want to try Europe anymore. I have recently heard this statement several times from others. He was hoping for a job in Dubai or the Emirates.

I immediately thought of Valli, my Swiss friend who lives on the other side of our local valley, so I can look over to him. Valli certainly has stardust in his blood, he traveled the world before settling down with his Berber wife and their two children in Hay Assersif. He did not settle down completely, because for a long period he has worked for a month at a time in Switzerland as a fine mechanic, where he has lived with his mother. The following month he spent with the family in our valley.

Half a year ago, when I met him, he told me that he had got a job in Dubai that he couldn't refuse, so after a short time the whole family steamed to Dubai.

Yet another statement that "paradise" Europe is fading. But it might also be good to get a little balance in things.

There are probably several reasons why Europe is fading. A major reason is certainly the war in Ukraine, which makes people insecure. What will happen on the day the war ends can be difficult to predict.

When I trudged home well loaded with a bottle of gas and a rucksack with various goods, I didn't get further than café Assersif, where I sat down in the shade and ordered a pot of tea.

Café Assersif is located at the bottom of the Hay Assersif valley with a nice view to the other side of the valley.

The road towards Paradise Valley at the bottom of the Hay Assersif valley

It looks as if the terrain rises from the valley floor all the way up to the top of the mountains, but it doesn't. When we try to go up the mountain road (in the distance on the picture) and down into the valley on the other side, we meet a parallel valley on our way.

I go over to this parallel valley once a month to pay our water bill. It takes place in a combined general store and payment office, where by now they know me quite well, due to the fact that I often pay the water in advance due to my trips to Europe.

The strange thing about this little valley is that they have started to create a city of the future here. A large municipal administration building has been built, which has not yet been put into use. A school has been built which is functioning well, and an assembly house has been built which I don't know how much they use. The mountain road past the buildings is cemented, so everything stands magnificent and fine and bears witness to the Morocco that King Mohamed VI wants it to be, even far out in the countryside. The city, the place, bears witness to the Morocco of the future.

Then the day came, when I have to pay the water bill, so let's go, with some water in the bottle.

We first have to go all the way down into the Hay Assersif valley to the oak (the dried-up river), where water only flows, when it rains in November and December. Then we have to go up the mountain road in the distance and down into the valley on the other side of this small mountain. Because on the other side of the small mountain or hill you see in the picture, you find the parallel valley.

So now we almost reached the top.

From the top we can look down into the next valley, the "valley of thefuture."

On the previous page you see the future valley, where we have the municipal administration building. The small building right next to it is the collection house.

Further down the road is the school and the general store, where I paid our waterbuill.

All in all, these measures testify to how strongly things are going in Morocco these years. When I see the school and the municipal administration building, I shouldn't be surprised if a petit l'hopital is

also being built before long - a small hospital that takes care of consultation, emergency cases and control of diseases including control of pregnant women and vaccinations.

On the way back to the Hay Assersif valley

We had such an old, small hospital in Aourir, where I received three of my corona vaccinations. It has just been demolished, and almost before the demolition was finished, they began to pour the foundations for a small new, modern hospital. It tingles my fingers, as many years ago, when I worked at Kalundborg Hospital, I was responsible for setting up and furnishing a new midwifery center and later represented the hospital during the construction of the new emergency room reception.

On the previous page, you see the new, small hospital in Aourir after 14 days of construction

My head could not escape the impressions of the day, so as I sat in my favorite place on the roof of the house in Hay Assersif, enjoying the magical light of the full moon over the mountains, I thought of all that had been initiated and accomplished in Morocco during my stay me here.

A highly distinctive project is a fantastic desert installation consisting of several rows of hollow mirrors, each of which collects the sun's rays and sends the rays towards a common point, whereby water is heated, evaporated and superheated. The superheated steam drives a turbine with a connected generator that supplies power to the Moroccan electricity grid.

"Traditional solar systems" have been and are being inaugurated.

The Moroccan government is also aware, that water can become a scarce commodity, so much has been done to collect water. A really good example is the large collection basins we have south of Agadir, which supply all of Agadir and the surrounding area with water, including us.

Deep wells are systematically dug from which the water is collected; 80 meters is not unusual. You can always see where these wells are located because of the associated water tower.

Large desalination plants that desalinate seawater are no exception either, I have seen on TV the king inaugurating such a plant.

All in all, Morocco is a country with many natural resources and potential. The Mediterranean and the Atlantic not to be forgotten! See the map on page 10! There are large fish stocks here, for the benefit of the Moroccan population and for export.

When flying to and from Agadir in daylight, you see large, shiny areas on the ground. These are greenhouses and plastic-covered areas to promote the growth of plants. There is no downtime here, cultivation and harvesting takes place throughout the year.

Jamila called: "Pål, come down from that roof, we're going to bed soon!" I got up and moved into the house. While I was lying in bed in the bedroom on the middle floor, waiting for Jamila, I fell asleep.

Earthquakes

I was suddenly awakened from sleep! It knocked and swayed and the house creaked. I lay perfectly still; I knew it was an earthquake. A thousand thoughts flew through my head! When will it stop? Has something happened, where is Jamila? How do we get out?

I looked at the clock; the time on 08/09 (2023) at 23:08 was burned into my memory.

Suddenly there was silence again, and at the same time Jamila came and shouted: "Out, out!" I was already on my way out of bed, so we both rushed into the salon, where I quickly grabbed my emergency backpack, which I always have ready. It contains passports, necessary personal papers, a change of clothes, payment cards and my medicine. Jamila had already taken her bag with similar contents from a closet in the bedroom.

Fortunately, we got out of the house safely, even though the power had gone out and we had no light. As I said, the gear is always clear, so we can take it in the dark. This is something we have learned after "our earthquake period" in Hassania.

When all the neighbors had come out, we sat down at a proper distance from the houses; the situation was calm. Everyone knew that another quake could come, so we armed ourselves with patience and made small talk.

As we sat there and I saw our joined together houses in silhouette, I knew at once why they are joined together! One house structurally supports the other, which is really smart in a situation like this!

Power came back on and some communicated with their relatives. The answers were both positive and negative, in some places it had gone well, in other places it had gone wrong. This is typical of the Berbers, it takes a lot to topple them, so everything still went smoothly.

It became much of the night outside; I ended up sleeping on two chairs; sat on one and rested his legs on the other. However, I was woken up by Jamila who suggested that we could sleep just inside the open front door, so that was it!

This Saturday morning I find that our village of Hay Assersif seems fortunately intact, as does Aourir, the town by the sea.

I see on TV that the earthquake has had a magnitude of 6.8 on the Richter scale with an epicenter about 70 km south of Marrakech, not more than a few hundred kilometers from us.

It is terrible to see all the damage that is in Marrakech and its surroundings, and then there are even several small mountain towns that the rescuers have not reached yet. We are the little ones in that game, these are huge powers!

We will not lie to ourselves; we know from experience that there may be more earthquakes within the next few days, so we must act accordingly. In Hassania we managed to count five earthquakes.

It's getting close to 7.30 pm and we've started getting ready for the night. I've never liked to take unnecessary chances, so I've made a bed right next to the front door, which doesn't need to be locked or closed; it must be clamped! I have counted steps and I know how to get out if the house is damaged and the power is cut off at the same time. The neighbor Mohamed has reported that he will sit outside and sleep in a chair tonight. It's just Jamila being cocky, she wants to sleep upstairs as usual; but she is also young and agile, so she can get down and out, even if the stairs or parts of the stairs should disappear. She jumps in the mountains like a goat without fear, she has tended sheep and goats there since she was a little girl. I am a big, heavy, old man who has never tended sheep and goats in the mountains.

I also have the backpack, the same one I took from the "emergency room" yesterday, standing by my side.

Fortunately, the night passed without further tremors, the only noise was Jamila, who had got cold feet and didn't want to sleep in the bedroom anyway. But since she is a proud Berber, she did not come downstairs to me; but arranged a bed outside the bedroom right by the stairs, so that she could slip out quickly if necessary.

Although the night has passed well, sad news greets me this morning, 10/9; more than 2000 people are reported dead, many injured and many, many homes destroyed.

I have also just been told by my friend Said, who lives on the other side of our mountain in Hafsi, where I have my workshop, studio and my small apartment, that unfortunately they in Hafsi have not escaped as easily as we in Hey Assertive. There are several minor damages; my tenancy should still be intact according to my friend and underling Hassan. I'll have to get over there and inspect the conditions myself when, hopefully, before long things will calm down a bit.

I was aware when I came down to my cafe in the trading town of Aourir yesterday that there might be problems with shopping because of the earthquake last night.

As expected, there were very few people in the otherwise busy city. People had stayed home to lick their wounds and look for home. There weren't many shops open either. The owners were scared at home to see the situation in the home and probably also expected only a few customers. I was lucky; I could buy bread at a small café, well enough at a premium, as the bread sellers didn't have any. The night's bakers had only baked very little because of the quake.

Today, the second day, there is still rationing on bread. I made an appointment with my bread seller, when I arrived in Aourir. He should reserve four loaves for me, if he got some. When I came back from the cafe, he had received very few; but anyway he had reserved four loaves for me.

As Aourir is still a shadow of its former self, fewer merchants than yesterday were open; but I just needed to buy some yogurt-like drink and I found the eggs at my honey man Hassan, who packaged them in shavings. Which Jamila complained about when I got home. I therefore asked her if she wanted eggs or not, as it had only been possible for me to get the eggs in the shavings.

It suddenly dawned on me that she doesn't understand the seriousness of the situation; Morocco is in a state of emergency where, in addition to the human tragedy, the production of goods and the distribution of the same goods are carried out according to a sparse pattern. We have to adjust to the fact, that we can't get what we want for the next while, even if we have money.

I want to see if I can come to Denmark and Sweden in 12 days, where I have some different appointments, meetings and activities. Jamila still doesn't want to go. I have therefore suggested that she go to Sister Essaddia in Tamraght, who has an old-fashioned Moroccan house, consisting of four sides with a patio (small space) in the middle. It is a house that is practical in times of earthquakes. But she won't! I can't be a witch, so I just have to hope for the best.

On the picture above, you can see the rubble from one of the few walls that did not survive the earthquake in Hafsi.

The night was again spent behind the front door, although I read that no more tremors are expected. The night also went well, without the blacksmith with the big sledgehammer waking us.

Today until morning, 11/09, Jamila and I have therefore lowered our preparedness to almost normal.

Already at 10 o'clock I rushed over to Hafsi, which I told about yesterday, to inspect. Fortunately, it was much better than I had dared to hope for after Said's statement. There was very little damage, a few old walls where the stones had rolled down. I also saw an entrance to a house where a temporary door section had been installed. There may well have been more minor injuries; I didn't go through the whole area. My workshop, studio and apartment were intact, although some cracks had appeared. I then proceeded down to Café Inou in Aourir to observe the daily ritual.

Believe it or not at the time of writing at 10.50, sitting outside the cafe,

I feel mini tremors, one person gets up and leaves, others stay seated and act like nothing, including myself. I have read that these mini tremors can last for some time and also know from our time in Hassania, where it took a few weeks before we were tremor free.

I have wondered a lot about house building in Morocco. It is large heavy concrete houses that are built, probably because they are easy to built and does not require great expertise; you have to be able to mix concrete, you have to be able to do some masonry, you have to be able to bind iron and you have to be able to cast. New thinking is needed, light flexible houses must be built, that can better withstand vibrations; I see some of these houses when I'm in Sweden, they could easily become modified models for houses here in Morocco, the only problem is that it requires a greater expertise to build them. But since this earthquake is unlikely to be the last, it is worth thinking about; it will be able to save many human lives when the big hammer is pounded.

We are getting ready for one more night and want to sleep under as normal conditions as possible. However, I refuse to lie down in bed in our first floor bedroom, the memory of the blacksmith with the big hammer is still too strong. I must have developed a phobia! I have instead chosen that I will sleep in one of the guest rooms on the ground floor with only my nightclothes on; it will be nice not to have to sleep like that again. Jamila can't quite make up her mind; she doesn't quite know where she wants to sleep.

Now we just hope and pray for a quiet night without destruction and banking.

Before we started the bed preparations, we had a visit from my nephew Talal. Jamila says she has no children; but now it is not quite right. She has Talal! Which she has bottled up from a very young age and brushed, cuddled and cared for, so there is a very close relationship between the two. It took a few years before I understood the strong bonds!

Talal works in the tourism industry and is employed at a very large all inclusive hotel.

He told how the hotel had been packed immediately before the earthquake; but now there were virtually no tourists left. It is understandable; but sad for Morocco; the old saying: "A misfortune seldom comes alone!" is valid forever.

We slept half an hour more, than we usually do, today, 12/09; these were good signs, for the night had passed quietly and without banking.

It is sad to read that the death toll has now exceeded 2,800, I wonder where we will end up?

In the midst of the tragedy, it pleases me that so many people are here organized. Networks have already been created where help is systematically offered for almost everything, you can also join the network yourself if there is something you are good at.

When I left the café, the report on TV captivated me to an uncanny degree. I was so moved by all the misery I saw with collapsed, totally obliterated houses, from which lifeless people were being carried out, that I forgot to pay for my tea. I got a little way up Aourir before I thought about it, so I rushed back to correct the mistake.

It is still easy to cross the road in Aourir, where it is normally quite difficult. It is not empty of people here, it will probably never be here either, but the throng of people is gone.

I see here and there a new kind of tourist, other than those who have just left the all inclusive hotels. The new tourists are wearing backpacks and will probably continue into the mountains to see and experience the tragedy. I have to state that there is a lot of difference between what my fellow human beings want to experience. Those who have just left us had wishes for sun, sea, food and drink in luxury surroundings. The new arrivals are not interested in luxury or in all-inclusive hotels, they want to experience the gloomy world on their own.

We went to bed as planned and everything breathed peace and quiet! On 13/7 just after midnight, I heard a real bump and feared the worst, the nerves were sitting outside on the nightclothes! But what was that? Fortunately, the bump was followed by a scraping sound; it was a couch

71

that was moved. I knew at once, that it was Jamila who had got cold feet again and didn't dare to sleep in the bedroom anymore, but wanted to sleep again in the salon outside close to the stairs, so she had moved one of the sofas all the way over to the stairs. After I complained about being woken up with bangs and bangs, I was still happy that it was just Jamila who had messed around, so we went back to bed. Jamila in her makeshift bed near the stairs and I in the guest room. The rest of the night was peaceful.

We could see from our roof terrace that our Wednesday souk (market close to where we live) was reduced probably because of the earthquake. We therefore discussed over breakfast whether I should go over there; we didn't lack much, so the result was that I went down to Aourir, where there is an alternative mini souk every Wednesday.

There are several reasons why this souk exists. At the big souk upstairs near us, you cannot buy live animals; you have to buy them at the mini souk in Aourir.

In addition, there are several vendors who do not have a car or other means of transportation, so it is much easier for them to come to Aourir, spread a cloth on the sidewalk or in the small square, to sell their wares that way.

In the picture on the next side, tomatoes are being dropped from a small truck. I bought two kg on the way to the café, which I paid DKK 3.50 for, as I had no idea if he was there when I got back.

There were only hens, roosters and turkeys for sale today. Rabbits, goats and sheep are also often sold.

The pictures show some of the vegetables and herbs that are sold.

The television is not working in the café today; the news flow about the earthquake has decreased. But I see in Morocco World News that our King Mohamed VI has visited the big hospital in Marrakech, where he has visited victims from the earthquake and donated a portion of blood. Again proof of his living, positive commitment to the Moroccan population.

But I'd better drink my tea so I can get on with today's program.

It was getting to be evening and we just had a visit from sister Habiba; it is she who is unmarried and in her mid-forties; but still extremely attractive. She lives alone in her father's home up in the Asrn mountains.

She was still quite shaken by the meeting with the blacksmith with the big hammer and told about how he had knocked loose on the fathers' home, so that everything flapped, but still it held. She had spent the night alone outside, and she had slept what she could at a proper distance from the houses. She had been having stomach problems almost ever since, it was only today that it felt better.

I have to go with list shoes when it comes to Habiba. Jamila wants to do everything as well as possible for her sister. When it comes to food;

I stay completely out of it. When it's other things, like for example the bed I just made for Habiba and the old sofas she needs, I have to take part in it. But suddenly, like lightning from a clear sky, Jamila can become jealous, like when I brought the mattress to Habiba's bed. I cannot rule out that I have feelings for Habiba; but must acknowledge in my quiet mind, that it does not work with two wives and certainly not two sisters. I am also an old boy.

I went back to bed in the guest room and feared the worst, it was still the 13th! Jamila laid down in her usual bed, where I believe she spent the whole night; At least I didn't hear any booms or bangs.

When I wanted to close the door to the guest room, I discovered that it couldn't be closed? I looked and could see that the door frame with the hinges had come out of alignment; I could also see that along the frame there was plaster, so now we have a memory of the earthquake; but it shouldn't surprise me if there are more coming down the road.

Our main water was shut off for the night, which I understand, as the earthquake has caused leaks in the piping system out in the ground. It is about limiting water consumption with the nightly closure. I also know from experience that they are quick to find the errors and fix them.

Although modern plastic pipes are everywhere, they occasionally burst due to the harsh soil conditions, so for that reason alone it has been difficult to withstand the earthquake.

I looked at my wristwatch! Ahhh! It was past midnight; it had become the 14/9, what a relief! It can be a bit difficult not to be superstitious, so I settled comfortably in bed and slept well despite the open door.

On 15/9 I sensed that the fear had subsided, and the situation with all the dead and injured, although not under control, was proceeding according to plan, so that when I went to my usual bed inside the bedroom in the evening, it was almost with peace of mind. Jamila didn't want to get into her bed in the bedroom anyway; but I must accept that; she must be allowed to nurture her phobia.

In the middle of the dark night I woke up! Now what was that?

75

Something bit or rather stabbed me in my left heel. I've tried it before, always in my feet, it feels like a bee sting! I checked the blankets and sheets again, there was nothing, it was the same pattern as before. It usually ticks a day's time; but disappears again, just dung annoying!

When I looked at our painted walls in the glow of the night lights, I suddenly saw small cracks in the wall. I found them to be new. They obviously don't come all at once; but comes creepingly. Wonder how many of these we have to deal with, and wonder how big they will be?

I took a picture of one of the cracks in the lower plane, as you see below.

It was difficult to photograph; but I still hope you can see the crack in the middle of the picture. It is unfortunately quite long, it is longer than the picture shows.

But not only that, when I wanted to use the toilet on the middle floor which I don't normally use, I found the door hard to close? Upon closer inspection, the frame was for this door also out of luck! Now I'm thinking, what will be the next thing that's hit crooked?!

After half an hour with a little supper and a pain-relieving tablet, I slept until the bright morning without dreaming about the small injuries; on the contrary, we are both infinitely grateful that we managed the earthquake so well!

It managed to stay on 16/9 and I managed to get hold of Rachid and an assistant Ahmed. It was today that we had to get all the gear out to Habiba in the Asrn mountains. There was the bed I had made, including the mattress I had bought and the old sofas with cushions, it filled the whole little truck that was loaded on the roof.

I hadn't been in Asrn long and was afraid of the dried up river bed, the oak, which I needn't have been, because a brand new bridge had been built which we crossed.

After driving on some difficult mountain roads we reached Habiba who was beaming like a little sun as we unloaded it all. She took part in the reading and fiddled with mattresses and sofas.

On the way home to Hay Assersif, Rachid and I got to talking about the world situation. I asked Rachid directly who won the war, by implication between Russia and their allies and Ukraine and their allies? He didn't really know how it was going to go, and as he chewed on the question a bit, I said, "It won't be Russia or Ukraine or any of their allies! It'll be those standing in the wings, frothing the cream while they watch , how the warring parties wear themselves out while profiting from all the goods they sell to them.

They increase their influence in all areas: Economy, ideology, technology, industry and prosperity. They are booming all over Southeast Asia, including China of course; well helped by rich Arab states."

I had listened well to the old hippie man, so I continued: "It will be strange for Europe to end up in second or third place. It will be

77

strange not to have to complain about the flow of refugees; it will be strange to have to do all the dirty work themselves: it will be strange to become a lesser tongue in the world's scales!"

Rachid, who is close friends with my friend, the philosopher Soufiane, is also not without philosophical skills and thinks a lot about life. He looked at me, then said: "It's not that bad, Pål! Because you Europeans have something, that many of the rest of us lack. You have the ability and tradition to plan for the future; you are good at taking the unforeseen into account events!"

I chewed a bit on what he had said and with my travels around the world as ballast, I had to prove him right! So old Europe, you are saved once again!

Rachid also has another hobby that he often brings to the track. It also happened now, as we rumbled off in the little truck. "Pål, it is a misconception that the world regards many terrorists as Muslims! A terrorist cannot be religious, neither Muslim nor Christian, nor have another religion. If you are a terrorist, you cannot observe either what is written in the Bible or in the Koran !" he said. He went on to tell specifically what was written in the holy books and ended by saying: "Pål, can't you try to explain it to them in Europe, Denmark and Sweden and wherever else you come." I of course promised Rachid to help with passing on the message once again!

It has finally reached 17/9 and the condition is so settled that it is allowed to joke a little again. As most Moroccans love jokes, I had one up my sleeve when I got into the Aktaff, that was going to drive me down to Aourir.

It was a relatively new driver who seemed to be awake, also joking and scared.

Since his old car had a starry windshield (probably stone chips), I told him, "Well, you must have been to Sweden!" At first he looked at me strangely, then he let out a raucous laugh and said: "Yes, I was in Stockholm last night, bang, bang!" It struck me a bit that he understood the joke so quickly, but again proof of how quickly the news media works in our new little world.

A few days have now passed since the tragic earthquake toppled large parts of Morocco.

We have to state that we now have two internal doors in our house, where the back frame has been bent so that the doors cannot be closed. The cracks we found in the kitchen wall have, as expected, become larger both in length and in width. We just hope there won't be any more.

It is also difficult to get certain goods in our trading town of Aourir. The shops, which are usually full of goods, have become somewhat sloppy. I have no idea if it's because of broken roads, factories that are closed, lack of labor or maybe a combination of all. We must arm ourselves with patience, watch the time and buy alternative goods.

We don't sleep very well either. We both wake countless times in the night, tossing and turning in a sweat, with the great blacksmith and his hammer in our thoughts. I feel like the time we were sailing with a ship in the Biscay, and we and we had to seek an emergency port in A Coruña. Although then it was not the great blacksmith with the hammer; but water, water and more water that gushed in, the feeling and sensation is the same. Fortunately, I have some good psychological courses as ballast. Courses that my old workplace Asnasvarket spent on me, so that I had the opportunity to support my employees in crisis situations. The tools from that time have helped me several times in my life, so they need to be used again.

It ended up being 19/9. When I got home from the café at about 1.30 pm and had eaten some leftover chicken from yesterday and devoured a bowl of Jamila's fruit ice cream, I laid down on the sofa on the top floor and looked up at the ceiling. Just before the eyes slid in, I became aware of a stripe on the ceiling; it was another crack that had seen the light of day! As I reasoned that it couldn't be otherwise, Jamila came dragging an old bag from a shopping cart she had pulled out of the storage room. When Jamila asked if we shouldn't scrap it, and I replied that we had decided that a long time ago, she immediately flipped it upside down and promptly jumped back! What was that though?! More than 10 little baby scorpions, scurrying around on the floor!

The hunting instinct was quickly ignited in Jamila, who caught up with one after the other, after which they had to let go.

When she sprinkled insect powder into the bag, a few more spilled out and suffered the same fate.

I mean knowing that scorpions give birth to live young so the possibility of them being born in the bag is there, so now the questions are just: Where is their mother? And how did she get up in a bag on the top floor to give birth to them? It's not so nice to know that she's on the loose!

While I was writing sitting on the roof, I occasionally looked at the neighboring houses and discovered a huge crack on the top of one of the houses, it must be added that the construction of the house is not top notch; yet.

I think that even though we have escaped unharmed, alive and with our homes and possessions intact, some of us will probably have to brace ourselves for future repairs to our houses.

It's tomorrow evening, if all goes well, I want to start my journey to Denmark and Sweden, so I'll go over to the apartment in Hafsi before it gets dark and sleep a bit, before my under-resident Hassan or his brother Abul Karim, drive me to the airport in Agadir at three inthe night, so I can be there at four; three hours before we have to fly to Bordeaux in France. From Bordeaux, the trip goes after a few hours to Kastrup, where I would like to be at half past five in the afternoon.

It will be a tough game. The six weeks I normally have available in the Nordic countries have been cut to two weeks, as Jamila is reluctant to let me go in the current situation. That's not how to be afraid. Instead, I will have to correct the stay on the next visit to Denmark and Sweden.

I honestly feel like a coward, I have guaranteed Jamila that there will be no more earthquakes here and now; it will be a very long time before one comes again, I explained to her. I can say no more about future earthquakes than my father could say about nuclear bombs, when he guaranteed me years ago that there would not be more atomic explosions. He must have had the same wretched feeling then that I have now.

Then I reached Agadir airport and am now sitting waiting for boarding in about an hour and a half. I was told yesterday that the all inclusive tourists have returned to the hotels in and around Agadir. But despite this, I discovered that people are much more affected by the earthquake than I expected. When I visited a good friend yesterday, all we talked about was the earthquake. His parents have a country house a little inland from here. Their buildings had withstood the hammer blows, while their neighbors' houses had sunk into rubble. My friend's wife, who is normally a bubbly young woman and mother of three little pods, two girls and a boy, was lying on the couch looking up at the ceiling? When I asked if she was sick, I was told that she was not feeling well after the earthquake, she was both scared and sad.

It is very strange, one of the first things I was introduced to when I came to the Nordics was the large landslide up north of Gothenburg in Sweden; it looks remarkably like earthquake damage; but fortunately it is very limited. I have to be careful not to get paranoid!

Western Sahara

Back in Morocco, I sat again in my favorite place on the flat roof of the house in the moonlight.

My thoughts revolved around the "socially just citizens" in Denmark who say: "Don't visit Morocco, because they have annexed Western Sahara!"

They have probably never been to Morocco because of their attitude, and for the same reason they have never visited Western Sahara. But they can make a statement about the conditions!

I also have no doubt that their statement is due to the UN's "allocation" of the area to the Polisario and not to the Kingdom of Morocco.

If we have that attitude, there are not many countries that we can visit and holiday in. Many of the countries of the world have or have had colonies and territories they enforce or enforced the right to and social conditions that we do not agree with.

Next, one should also assess whether the state or conditions that prevail in an area with its current government are better than it would have been with another government in place. The rulers of the "knowing world" have always divided the world in solemn conventions and solemn agreements, and look what has come of the divisions in North

Africa and elsewhere after World War II?!

Knowing that it was decided by the UN in 1975 that Western Sahara should be a Saharawi state, with a Saharawi government, I still allow myself to dig into the conditions.

I am passionate about clarifying a number of questions: Has there ever been a unified state in the area? How is the population composed? Has the area been inhabited in its entirety or only in specific places? How is it related to culture and language?

I am wondering how I best to get information about these matters. Danish texts are somewhat scarce; I sense that French and English descriptions are the most complete. I will also draw heavily on the statements of my friends. The historian must know a lot about the conditions and the lawyer must also know a lot.

I'm quite clear in my head! I have read a lot, and my historical friend has not held back, just as the jurist has also made his contribution; if I wrote everything down straight away it would fill a small book! So what do I do? I try to make a relevant summary of it all.

Western Sahara was not so terribly many years ago in historical time, 500 years before our era, not a desert; but a savanna area with nomads and their grazing cattle. The area was not a nation and never has been a nation. It consisted of tribal communities, Phoenicians and later Romans.

The Phoenicians were already there in the 5th century BC; they probably had colonies on the coast, just as the Romans did later. There was an Arab invasion from the west in the 8th century, which meant that the residents of the area became Muslim and that the area was at the same time characterized by Arab culture. As the years went by, the area became more and more a desert. It ended up with the desert we see today. The result was a low-developed area, although over the years there have also been routes for desert caravans from Africa to North Africa through the area.

The 11th century saw a number of wars between the population of the

83

area and tribes from neighboring areas.

In 1884, Spain settled on a large part of the Western Sahara. In 1958 they expanded and joined the occupied territories together, so that it became the Spanish Western Sahara - Rio del Oro.

Polisario, the movement for a Saharawi state, was formed by students and former soldiers of the Spanish army in Western Sahara in 1973. Algeria, Morocco's old arch-enemy, allegedly had a hand in the game and continues to sponsor Polisario.

In late 1975, Spain held meetings with the leader of the Polisario to negotiate the terms of a handover of Western Sahara to the Polisario. Almost at the same time, Morocco and Mauritania began to stir and made Spain aware that the Western Sahara was a historical part of their territories. See the map page 10.

It wasn't really the people who were being heard, it was only the Polisario! The rebel movement! Because of its marking. Not many people think about that!

It must be added that over time the Berbers who originally inhabited the Western Sahara were mixed with tribes from surrounding areas, and the result was the Saharawi people we see today.

Morocco brought the case to the UN, arguing that the area rightfully belonged to them due to the (Berber) population's ties to Morocco; The UN came to the conclusion that although there were ties with Morocco, they were insufficient, so as Western Sahara was a land owned by no one, the land should belong to its inhabitants; since there was no one but Polisario to form a government, Polisario had to do this, basta!

Mauritania gave up rather quickly when the problems arose.

In November of that year, 300,000 unarmed Moroccans marched into the Sahara and crossed the Western Sahara at the behest of King Hassan II. It is this march that is known as the Green March.

Morocco then annexed ⅔ of the area in 1976 and the rest in 1979.

On 27 February 1976, the Polisario declared the Saharawi Arab

Democratic Republic-SADR, forming a government-in-exile and starting a guerilla war against Morocco that continued until 1991, when it was agreed that a referendum should be held to decide whether Western Sahara should belong to the Saharawis (Polisario) or Morocco. However, at the time of writing, the vote has not yet been held, due to several different circumstances.

The status today is that Morocco has built sand embankments with barbed wire to protect the area.

The area has a lot of fishing from the Atlantic Ocean and mining - phosphates.

Of course, I have also given myself some continuous thoughts about the whole thing.

Morocco already consists of a patchwork of areas, different landscapes and people, so in that way Western Sahara is a natural extension, both geographically and population-wise, of Morocco.

I also wonder how much of a part Algeria has in the formation of the Polisario? Algeria, with its socialist friends, has a great interest in the Western Sahara, naturally, as does Morocco and its allies.

It is Morocco that is delaying a referendum, and I understand why! It is almost a law of nature that when people have a choice and have to vote, they vote for a head of state who is not a king. The king is considered as a sole ruler, no matter how many and good intentions he has. He is perceived as an old-fashioned institution. Conversely, the president, the head of state, is considered freedom, even if he just represents a one-party system. It is absolutely not a given that a head of state is democratic or has democratic wishes. So I want to say: "Better a good and just king than a dubious president as the head of state!"

One forgets; it was not the people who were heard, it was only the Polisario! Did they even have the support of the entire population? What mandate did the Polisario have to represent Western Sahara. Polisario was, as I said, founded by students and local soldiers from the Spanish army. It is always easy to stand with a wronged, raised index finger!

I think that the case was processed per routine of the United Nations. Why didn't the UN do more thorough work and make proposals for negotiation? It is all too easy as a big brother to choose the quick, probate solution!

In the course of time, I have talked with Indian rebels in Chiapas province in Mexico. I have spoken to the basic rebel movement and I have been to Northern Cyprus and seen the conditions there. Everywhere I met friendly, committed people who were passionate about their cause.

I almost ended up in the tub because of my visit to Northern Cyprus. A few years after my visit there, I was with my then wife Runa on holiday in Cyprus (south). We took part in a sailing trip up the coast, past the demarcation line. Just across the line were several large empty luxury hotels; I had seen them before.

It set off a pure flow of words from the Cypriot skipper's English wife. She told us about the terrible conditions that prevailed in Northern Cyprus!

Being the old provocateur that I am, I said out loud that I couldn't understand that?

I further explained that I had been there two years ago, where I had experienced friendly people in a well-functioning society. There had been plenty to eat and drink. I had been to a café, a restaurant and the bank; everything was top notch; it worked! I couldn't say more! The woman took me by one arm and the man took me by the other; they wanted to throw me overboard! Luckily some of the tourists came to my rescue while Runa screamed loudly! The rest of the sailing trip to Aiya Napa took place in a very pressurized atmosphere.

You rarely get rich from injury; but clever! Should I find myself in a similar situation in my future career, I must keep my mouth shut!

Conclusion; I have had my questions clarified: Western Sahara has never been a united nation. The population, whatever they are called, has Berber roots with mixed blood from outside. The area has not been inhabited evenly throughout; but only in specific places; with the largest population out by the coast. Culture and language are both mixtures, as the area had both Morocco, Mauritania and Algeria as neighbors, so Hassaniya, a variant of Arabic, dominates. In addition, languages from Africa south of the Western Sahara and a few different Berber languages are spoken. Brother-in-law Mohamed, who is Berber, and who fishes both from Tarfaya and Dakhla, see map page 10, claims that he communicates well with the population, so some Berber language is spoken. He has also reported that you still get a long way with Spanish, especially out on the coast.

Not so long ago I was lucky enough to meet a man who came from Tarfaya and curious as I was, I naturally asked him about the conditions in the Western Sahara. He openly shared that he was happy to live there and thrived. He also said that although the Polisario still exists and "rattles the sabers" in between, their "sabre rattling" was getting longer and longer.

Then, when I ventured to bring my conclusion – my view of the whole Western Sahara situation, he could not help but applaud my explanation. He knew very well that people, he even said all people in this world, chased democracy at any cost without thinking and understanding the consequences. He added something that I often think about myself. He said: "The most important thing is that the individual person feels free, and since the feeling of freedom is a personal feeling, it doesn't matter whether you live in a kingdom or a democracy, just that the framework for the feeling of freedom is present.

So I sincerely hope that both the people of Western Sahara, the rest of the world and the UN become aware of the sympathetic and right-thinking king who rules Western Sahara - a king who has shown and continues to show his good will to unite everyone in his kingdom and at the same time works to ensure that everyone has a high standard of living with a high level of personal freedom.

Daily life in Morocco

I have told everything and everyone, family, relatives and friends, that when I die, I will be buried where I die. This is my attitude as the citizen of the world I hope I am.

So when I proclaimed this to Soufiane, he looked at me and said, "Well if you die in Morocco, you can't just be buried here; it requires an addendum to your will!" It came quite behind me; but I knew very well that he, as a lawyer, knew what he was talking about. So the end of it all was that he promised me to contact a lawyer friend who had an office over in the other street, Rue de Imiki.

The end of it all was that Soufiane was able to reserve a time for my venture, so that both Soufiane and I made the pilgrimage there on time.

The lawyer, a man in his late thirties, was of course Berber, but still rather large with a broad grin and narrow, slanted, smiling eyes.

Soufiane was also a translator, as the lawyer strangely spoke neither English nor French.

I explained that if I were to die in Morocco, I would be laid to rest in the cemetery over on the other side of the Hay Assersif valley, so that I can lie and look at my beloved valley and my beloved home.

I also told, that I have tried to talk to Jamila about it; but it doesn't work, she gets sick; Poul lives forever, so I'm going to tighten my balls and keep going.

There is a difference between lawyers in Denmark and in Sweden. But the difference between the lawyers in these two countries and in Morocco is even greater. The Moroccan lawyers live in a world of their own.

Everything became neat with Arabic intricate letters per manually written into a journal, where all previous cases were also noted. Soufiane and I then signed off with names, clarification and signature.

Subsequently, the lawyer created a file on his computer and began painstakingly entering the document. Once this was completed and the document printed, Soufiane and I had to sign again, after which I was told that it would take approximately 14 days before the papers would be ready.

In the end I paid the equivalent of DKK 700. I could be allowed to split the amount or wait to pay it. As I had expected a sum in that direction, I took the bills out of my pocket and paid him the whole.

It wasn't just law that we managed to discuss. They saw my new website and my books and asked a lot about them. Soufiane naturally knew quite a bit in advance; but to the lawyer it was new.

My previous statements in this book about the distribution of Berbers and Arabs in Morocco came up for discussion, so I had to greet you from both and say that the distribution figures are wrong, because in Morocco the vast majority are Berbers. The Arab population appears in too large a number due to the fact that if a person speaks Dahia, he or she is counted as an Arab. The statement must be at Soufiane's and the lawyer's own expense.

Of course, we also discussed Western Sahara, Polisario and Hamas. I must admit that our views, opinions and considerations were fairly similar. But in that connection I should also remember to tell you that Morocco had once been a huge country that had started at the Mediterranean and had gone all the way down along the Atlantic Ocean, including the Western Sahara to what is today called Senegal. This statement must also be at the expense of the two lawyers.

When I made a provocative statement during the meeting, both immediately rejected the claim. I claimed that in just a few years Morocco would introduce the Latin letters instead of the Arabic letters. "That would never happen!" they both claimed.

I explained what they already knew, how Atstürk had modernized Turkey many years ago, just as King Mohamed VI is doing in Morocco now. Modernization had also brought about a change between Arabic, intricate letters and Latin simple letters.

I went on to explain how the Morocco I came to 11 years ago had drastically evolved into a modern country. I knew very well that the Arabic letters and the Koran are connected; but I claimed that if the Turks could make it work, so could they.

Furthermore, I claimed that the Latin letters must be much easier to handle in the computer; this claim was probably my own.

After this argument there was silence for a while, after which Soufiane was the first to open his mouth and say that it was not at all improbable that it would turn out that way. The prosecutor had to rule him out. But thought the letters of the Berbers were just as good. I had to agree with him, but added that if you were smart, you shouldn't try something new and untried. A large part of the world uses the Latin letters or something similar, I explained further. As always, discussion was matter-of-fact and took place in a calm manner.

As we went down the stairs, Soufiane said with a wry smile, "Rachid's not here anymore!" I thought the worst, that he was dead! But luckily Soufiane continued: "He's in Düsseldorf, Germany today and hasn't been in Morocco for three days. Tomorrow he's going on to Dortmund where he's got a three-month work and stay contract, so we'll see where well he's doing there. Maybe he'll stay in Germany."

I knew very well that he had contacts in Germany; but still, that he had gone off so soon struck me.

"We will miss him." Soufiane concluded. I can only agree with him in this statement.

On the way home, I passed by Abdullah, who had sewn covers for the three sofas and cushion covers for eight cushions. The covers for the sofas and cushions were of the same type of fabric, so that for once we could have the same cushions and covers. I got the entire pier for the three sofas and eight cushions for the equivalent of DKK 756. I was even offered to eat with them, but I declined as I was on my way home to Jamila.

A few days ago in the evening the temperature dropped a bit, and clouds appeared in the sky. I sat outside and enjoyed the slightly weaker air and sure if I didn't also get 3 drops of rain on me. We both agreed that now it was getting colder and maybe rainy - nice - wonderful! But alas, in the middle of the night the heat returned and spoiled sleep. The next day was just a little colder than the days before; but still above 30 degrees.

Again last night the clouds gathered in the sky; now it happened! But the night was again a nightmare with difficulty sleeping. The hot nights are not good for my arthritis. Even though I don't have much arthritis, it still happens that I throw off the blanket and the faint breeze passing my skin brings out the arthritis in the underlying muscles.

Our new resident slept outside on a blanket last night; but seem to have coped quite well, both father, mother and their little daughter. I thought back to the time I sailed the tropics on an iron ship when the air conditioner broke down. Back then I slept on the deck at night, so maybe in the coming night I would have to move up to the roof top?!

It wasn't just sleeping on the roof; as an old man I didn't just want to sleep on a blanket on the hard tiles but had to have a bed and we had just given all our extra beds to Habiba so time passed and we got to 19/10 where it was warm, although the night was not scorching.

In the middle of the night I heard it fiddling and thought it was the neighbor who couldn't sleep. It sometimes happens that he is active most of the night.

When I asked Jamila in the morning if she had heard the crazy neighbor going around all night, she replied that for once it wasn't him. "It had rained!" she continued.

I couldn't believe my eyes and went up to the terrace, where I found that it was good enough.

Although the temperature had changed from 30 degrees to 24 degrees, the sky was still a lovely blue today, so the morning exercise trip down through Aourir was a delight in the pleasant climate.

I have to state that the rain came exactly on time, and that the temperature is quite normal, which is worth thinking about in the climate-deviant times.

There were plenty of puddles, and a way around them had to be found. When it hasn't rained for so long, it's as if the ground isn't prepared for the rain.

A huge puddle.

The exercise tour ended like most times at café Inou (that means my café in Tamazight), where I had my usual tea with nana (mint).

Back home, I have just washed and hung up the laundry on the upper roof terrace. It's the old story that I'm the best at getting the soap residue out of the clothes on our simple washing machine. It's easy enough, just plenty of rinsing water. But it can be difficult when you, like Jamila, has been told since childhood that water is precious, so you have to save on it.

As always, after hanging up the laundry, I sat on the chair and looked at the yellow and orange hillsides and the houses of the village.

In the valley on our side I saw a goat herder with a sack on his neck. Wondering what he picked up this time of year? In any case, it wasn't almonds, which will later become part of; maybe it was olives he stuffed in his sack.

I actually had my mystery solved the following day when the goatherd stood in the small square in Aourir with two open plastic sacks full of olives that he was trying to sell.

Today, 22/10-2023, is a special day to wake up to, with heavy black clouds hanging low over the mountains and a temperature of just 18 degrees - and rain. I know everyone is happy and hoping that the rain will continue, because that means good natural crops of lots and lots. What we particularly focus on are olives and argan. Argan oil is a famous Moroccan oil. It is said that it is only found in Morocco, but I have been told that there should also be some in Mexico. Argan oil has recently reached astronomical heights in terms of price and many stores that normally sell it no longer carry it.

In times of normal prices, it is used in exclusive cooking - enters the body and gives the skin a special shine. But it is in the cosmetic industry that it is used the most, partly mixed with cosmetic products and partly directly as an oil that is either smeared or sprayed on the skin. The argan oil is usually considered to be a good source of income for Morocco.

It rained so much today that after a few days of waiting we will see our valley in its green clothing. It is strange to think that all the green growths that will magically appear are hidden in the orange-brown hard soil of the mountains.

Apropos the hard ground, I don't understand that our mountains are long gone, because today 23/10, when I simply had to get out of the enclosure, I managed to escape between two downpours and pass all that material up from the mountains - sand, gravel and small pieces of rock that the rain had taken from them. It is large quantities that wash down, and the sum of these quantities must become very large over time.

I just made it to the cafe before the rain started again. So now I'm sitting outside under the half roof and watching the rain and drenched people while my tired red, eyes burn and my left foot feels like it was burned by not just one "Danish" fire pit; but several "Danish" fire pits.

It requires an explanation. As always, when the weather changes and the temperature drops, we have to go back to the big blankets at night. Usually the carpets are hung out in the sun, so that it can burn all the vermin out of them. Due to the rain this could not be done this time, so we used the blankets as they were.

Suddenly between four and five o'clock this morning I awoke abruptly; I was stung on the top of my left foot exactly as explained earlier. I rushed out to wash the foot, disinfect it and oil it. But the damage had been done, it already stung and tingled badly, so even though I tried to sleep afterwards, it didn't lead to much sleep. Jamila had also woken up and didn't sleep much because of me either, so already at a little past six we got up and started the day's activities.

I was lucky, I found the old roll on stick against insect bites from Sweden at the top of a cupboard, luckily it alleviated the stinging quite a bit.

As I wrote earlier, I have experienced it several times before, and Jamila has also tried it. We get stung by something in the morning, usually on the feet or lower legs, after which it stings and tingles all day. What it is that stings us, I have no idea, there is nothing to see in the carpet after a bite. Jamila claims that they are small spiders - predatory spiders, which is why, she even showed me what they look like. Where she got it from, I don't know; but I must suppose that it is not altogether improbable.

94

I must confess that I was more carried away by the bite yesterday than I had expected. The Swedish conditioner only helped for a while. I had a hard time keeping calm, even though I was terribly tired. I tried several times to lie down on the couch; but it was only for a short time each time; then stuck the "needle" into the foot again, so I went up with a thud! The calf muscle on the same leg started cramping, which did not improve the situation.

At one point it was dizzying for me, so I had to try to stay calm despite the turmoil.

Later I managed to consult the Internet. When I look at the spiders that Jamila thinks are the cause of our bites and compare them to tarantulas, the similarity is great, so without being too sure, I assume that it is tarantulas that have invaded our area and our house. Moreover, they should be harmless to a normal, healthy person, even if their sting and the after-effects are far from pleasant. If I had been good at dancing, I would have danced the tarantella to get rid of the anxiety.

I read further that you have to disinfect the plug; I had done that last night with Betadin, which is an excellent Moroccan disinfectant, so my intuition had not been entirely wrong.

Now I wonder how the night will go? I have some painkillers I'd rather not take; but for once I dare to take one of them, hoping that it will dull the stinging in the foot, and make the calf muscle relax. But neither Jamila nor I want to go to bed tonight. It will be the sofas or one of the guest rooms.

Jamila has many different things in the bedroom; the wardrobes are full of clothes; there are piles of old clothes that I have long said we should throw out. But you never know, "maybe brother Hassan, sister Habiba or brother-in-law Mohamed can use some of it one day!" says Jamila, so we have to wait to throw it out.

I am really afraid that it will turn into nests of vermin, so after my sting I offered to throw it all out. But I wasn't allowed to do that, it's Jamila herself who has to speak out. She circles the hot porridge like the cat; but has not started yet. It takes time to decide - things take time!

I laid down on the sofa on the middle floor as a start, while Jamila laid down on her favorite sofa on the top floor.

For once I slept without problems, when I woke up a little groggy after a few hours, I went down to a guest room and slept on; it didn't sting my foot anymore, now it just tingled, it was tolerable, so now I could sleep on and woke up in the morning, overslept at 9. What a relief!

It also rained last night and there are clouds in the sky, so now we'll have to see what happens. There is a lot of mud in the streets and squares; the fishmonger has laid out fish boxes (plastic boxes) with the bottom in the air, so that you can step on them to reach the counter, so it's about keeping your balance!

It's incredible how happy everyone is about the rain. When I say, "It's been raining quite a bit." they smile, nod and say: "Alham du Lillah!" Translated, it means: "God be praised!"

By the way, I just met Vali, my friend from Switzerland, who lives on the other side of the valley. When I asked him how the work in Dubai went, he replied that he had not been to Dubai; but in Kuwait to maintain and repair gas turbines; he also looks remarkably like one of the Swiss turbine fitters I have known so many of from my past at the power station. He was beaming like the sun, the coffers were full, it was a lot of money he had scooped up during the time he had worked in Kuwait. In 5 days Switzerland called again. This time it wasn't as a repairman at a cookie factory; it was in a chocolate factory.

A few days ago, Jamila came home and said that she had seen a man who had fallen from a building permit; she thought he was dead. It wasn't something she was deeply moved about. There are so many who are injured in construction and in industry because of a completely different safety than the one we are used to; it is sad; but again things take time! It is a whole attitude to life that needs to be changed. You can gradually buy many security items in the well-stocked shops; but few buy them.

Then when we had to redo our kitchen drain upstairs and the floor had to be chipped and chipped and the contractor Jamila insisted on doing the job and got down to business, I objected and said she should wear safety glasses and maybe a mask. It would probably work, she had chopped with the chisel so many times before without anything happening. What happened? She got a bit of the material in her eye - not much - but enough for her to understand the seriousness of what I had said, so we postponed the work for a day, so that I could go down to Hassan's hardware store and buy protective glasses, a mask and hearing protection. So today, with joint help, we got the trench cut. I had to step in with the angle grinder to get through the tiles and the concrete layer. Now I just need to have some formwork done so that Jamila can mold around the pipe, so that we can hide it in a slightly wider doorway than the existing one.

Today, 5/11, it was cloudy this morning and half-cold, below 18 degrees C; now here at 12 o'clock the temperature is just 22 degrees, although it has cleared up. Jamila says it's Swedish weather; I don't quite agree with her. I just spoke to my old friend Mogens back home in Denmark, who explained that the weather was bad and that it was only 9 degrees C, so there is a difference.

I see more and more caravans in pitches, on the road and on the street. The time for them is now; they invade Morocco every year where they settle. Some stay out in nature at the beach and some in the mountains, and they are rarely rejected, as long as they behave properly and don't screw up.

We have a 'German' campsite in Hay Assersif a few kilometers from where we live. There are also many who live here. It is the ideal place for this kind of tourist, where they can live in the shelter of the mountains. We watch them from our terrace pass by on our little 'main road' towards Paradise Valley. Most are pensioners, many from France, some from Germany and Sweden. Strangely enough, there are almost never Danish caravans among the passers-by.

The backpackers have also made their inroads. Although they are very similar to the "disaster tourists" who came after the earthquake, there is still a difference. They rent in small hotels, privately or live in tents on the campsites. Private rental is quite easy. It's just to sit down in a café, start talking a little and find someone who speaks French or maybe English if French doesn't work. As previously written, it is the young people who speak English, so it is just a matter of finding a young intelligent person and asking about private accommodation. There are also some who stand and wave their keys along the roads; it means they have rooms for rent.

There are always tourists at the big all inclusive hotels along Aourir beach - called Banana Beach and further on in Tamraght, Targszout and further up the coast and of course along the big beach in Agadir.

I can see that the big hotels have eaten away at the small guesthouses in Tamragh. Where before it was almost always fully booked, there are now more available rooms for rent.

But luckily we have the surfers who invade Aourir - Tamraght and Tagsazout, called Surfers Paradise, in the winter months. In Surfers Paradise, the big waves roll towards the coast from the huge Atlantic Ocean. These people are not interested in a luxury holiday at one of the exclusive hotels; they only have one passion - surfing, so luckily they keep the small guesthouses and the small surfing hotels going. Surfer hotels are also guest houses that have made surfing their specialty - storage of surfing boards and transport every day to and from the beach - comfortable accommodation and usually 2 meals a day. The drinks are usually in a fridge, from which they can be taken for a fee.

I have just been to a business with office supplies and such, where they also do printing. I got to talk to the lady in the shop, who told me that she actually had the job out of necessity; she had a high diploma from the University of Agadir. She believed that it was because she was a woman that it was more difficult to get qualified, relevant work.

I have previously told you a little about my view of the position of women in Morocco, and I hope that you remember what I said, therefore I think that what she says is both right and wrong.

In everyday life, I see many women on the move also in "high" jobs, so women are not excluded from these jobs in any case; but it is probably true that it is more difficult to get a job as a woman in Morocco, like so many other places in the world.

In general, many more academics are trained in Morocco than are needed here and now; but I guess it's not bad; it shows, firstly, that the possibility of obtaining a high education is present, and secondly, it increases the sum of the country's knowledge.

The hope is that it will succeed in getting the wheels moving so much that there will be room for all these educated people. I personally believe that it will probably succeed when I look back on the eleven years I have lived here. There is a world of difference from when I first arrived in 2012 to today in 2023!

The vast majority of women out here in the province where I live wear the scarf that many in our Nordic countries associate with oppression. I've said before that it's actually a lot more complicated than that. When I think of my wife Jamila, I have one more explanation.

Jamila went with me to Sweden, got a residence permit and had to be Swedish. She took off her scarf and dressed like a Swedish woman; but she suffered - at the time I didn't know how much, I didn't understand the situation at all as I understand it today, where I stand with one foot in both camps.

Jamila carried her culture with her in her backpack - some would say: "And her religion!" Yes, both, Jamila is not particularly religious; but since religion and culture are connected, I cannot reject the claim entirely; but in any case the culture played an incredible role for her, she had been used to wearing the scarf from childhood, she had been used to being able to hide behind it, and take it up to her mouth for practical reasons in the dust storms when she guarded the family's goats and sheep in the mountains, and when she felt insecure.

So Jamila failed in Sweden - she suffered and I suffered! I therefore suggested to her several times that we should go back to Morocco; she rejected it, she had her pride; her family had told her that Sweden was paradise.

I was in Morocco alone visiting the family, Jamila didn't want to go. Subsequently, when I opened my eyes to her situation and recognized it, I almost forced her to go to Morocco. I had a plan in my head. She should not be Swedish, it would in the long run destroy her more than it had already destroyed her, my heart cried!

I had a little "money on the book" (sailor's language), so I set about finding a suitable home for us - after a while it turned out to be the house where we live now in the mountain village of Hay Assersif. I was quite aware that my future life would be hectic, as I also needed to spend a lot of time in Denmark and Sweden. But I saw no other option to solve the problem.

Fortunately, today I can state that my solution has borne fruit, although it has taken time for Jamila to find herself again. She has been transformed into the happy Jamila. She realizes that it was wrong of her to deny her culture; she recognizes that it is in the mountains of Morocco that she belongs, and she uses her scarf diligently again without thinking about it. She eats and she smiles and I'm happy about it.

It is much easier for me to adapt to all the different conditions and cultures I live with than it was for her with the "trial in Sweden." Don't forget I have stardust in my blood!

Milton Keynes UK
Ingram Content Group UK Ltd.
UKHW040845131024
449481UK00004B/203